The Haunted House

"*The Haunted House* is of the utmost significance
for anyone interested in exploring the
genius of Charles Dickens."
Peter Ackroyd

"Dickens's figures belong to poetry, like figures of
Dante or Shakespeare, in that a single phrase,
either by them or about them, may be enough
to set them wholly before us."
T.S. Eliot

"Dickens issued to the world more political and social
truths than have been uttered by all the professional
politicians, publicists and moralists
put together."
Karl Marx

"All his characters are my personal friends –
I am constantly comparing them with
living persons, and living persons with them."
Leo Tolstoy

ALMA CLASSICS

The Haunted House

Charles Dickens

with

Hesba Stretton
George Augustus Sala
Adelaide Anne Procter
Wilkie Collins
Elizabeth Gaskell

ALMA CLASSICS

ALMA CLASSICS LTD
Hogarth House
32-34 Paradise Road
Richmond
Surrey TW9 1SE
United Kingdom
www.almaclassics.com

The Haunted House first published in 1862
First published by Alma Classics Limited (previously Oneworld Classics
Limited) in 2009. Reprinted 2011.
This new edition first published by Alma Classics Ltd in 2015
Front cover image © Paul M. King Photography

Printed in Great Britain by CPI Group (UK) Ltd, Croydon CR0 4YY

ISBN: 978-1-84749-433-7

Contents

Charles Dickens (1812–70)

John Dickens,
Charles's father

Elizabeth Dickens,
Charles's mother

Catherine Dickens,
Charles's wife

Ellen Ternan

1 Mile End Terrace, Portsmouth, Dickens's birthplace (above left),
48 Doughty Street, London, Dickens's home 1837–39 (above right)
and Tavistock House, London, Dickens's residence 1851–60 (below)

Gad's Hill Place, Kent, where Dickens lived from 1857 to 1870 (above)
and the author in his study at Gad's Hill Place (below)

The Haunted House

1

The Mortals in the House

by Charles Dickens

U NDER NONE OF the accredited ghostly circumstances, and environed by none of the conventional ghostly surroundings, did I first make acquaintance with the house which is the subject of this Christmas piece. I saw it in daylight, with the sun upon it. There was no wind, no rain, no lightning, no thunder, no awful or unwonted circumstance of any kind to heighten its effect. More than that, I had come to it direct from a railway station – it was not more than a mile distant from the railway station – and, as I stood outside the house, looking back upon the way I had come, I could see the goods train running smoothly along the embankment in the valley. I will not say that everything was utterly commonplace, because I doubt if anything can be that, except to utterly commonplace people – and there my vanity steps in, but I will take it on myself to say that anybody might see the house as I saw it, any fine autumn morning.

The manner of my lighting on it was this.

I was travelling towards London out of the north, intending to stop by the way to look at the house. My health required a temporary residence in the country, and a friend of mine who knew that, and who had happened to drive past the house, had written to me to suggest it as a likely place. I had got into the train at midnight, and had fallen asleep, and had woke up and had sat looking out of the window at the brilliant Northern Lights in the sky, and had fallen asleep again, and had woke up again to find the night gone, with the usual discontented conviction on me that I hadn't been to sleep at all – upon which question, in the first imbecility of that condition, I am ashamed to believe that I would have done wager by battle with the man who sat opposite me. That opposite man had had, through the night – as that opposite man always has – several legs too many, and all of them too long. In addition to this unreasonable conduct (which was only to be expected of him), he had

had a pencil and a pocketbook, and had been perpetually listening and taking notes. It had appeared to me that these aggravating notes related to the jolts and bumps of the carriage, and I should have resigned myself to his taking them, under a general supposition that he was in the civil-engineering way of life, if he had not sat staring straight over my head whenever he listened. He was a goggle-eyed gentleman of a perplexed aspect, and his demeanour became unbearable.

It was a cold, dead morning (the sun not being up yet), and when I had out-watched the paling light of the fires of the iron country, and the curtain of heavy smoke that hung at once between me and the stars and between me and the day, I turned to my fellow traveller and said:

"I *beg* your pardon, sir, but do you observe anything particular in me?" For, really, he appeared to be taking down either my travelling cap or my hair, with a minuteness that was a liberty.

The goggle-eyed gentleman withdrew his eyes from behind me, as if the back of the carriage were a hundred miles off, and said, with a lofty look of compassion for my insignificance:

"In you, sir?... B."

"B, sir?" said I, growing warm.

"I have nothing to do with you, sir," returned the gentleman; "pray let me listen... O."

He enunciated this vowel after a pause, and noted it down.

At first I was alarmed, for an express lunatic and no communication with the guard is a serious position. The thought came to my relief that the gentleman might be what is popularly called a rapper: one of a sect for (some of) whom I have the highest respect, but whom I don't believe in. I was going to ask him the question, when he took the bread out of my mouth.

"You will excuse me," said the gentleman contemptuously, "if I am too much in advance of common humanity to trouble myself at all about it. I have passed the night – as indeed I pass the whole of my time now – in spiritual intercourse."

"Oh!" said I, something snappishly.

"The conference of the night began," continued the gentleman, turning several leaves of his notebook, "with this message: 'Evil communications corrupt good manners'."

"Sound," said I, "but, absolutely new?"

"New from spirits," returned the gentleman.

I could only repeat my rather snappish "Oh!" and ask if I might be favoured with the last communication?

"'A bird in the hand,'" said the gentleman, reading his last entry with great solemnity, "'is worth two in the Bosh.'"

"Truly I am of the same opinion," said I, "but shouldn't it be Bush?"

"It came to me, Bosh," returned the gentleman.

The gentleman then informed me that the spirit of Socrates had delivered this special revelation in the course of the night. "My friend, I hope you are pretty well. There are two in this railway carriage. How do you do? There are 17,479 spirits here, but you cannot see them. Pythagoras is here. He is not at liberty to mention it, but hopes you like travelling." Galileo had likewise dropped in, with this scientific intelligence. "I am glad to see you, *amico. Come sta?* Water will freeze when it is cold enough. *Addio!*" In the course of the night, also, the following phenomena had occurred. Bishop Butler had insisted on spelling his name "Bubler", for which offence against orthography and good manners he had been dismissed as out of temper. John Milton (suspected of wilful mystification) had repudiated the authorship of *Paradise Lost*, and had introduced, as joint authors of that poem, two unknown gentlemen, respectively named Grungers and Scadgingtone. And Prince Arthur, nephew of King John of England, had described himself as tolerably comfortable in the seventh circle, where he was learning to paint on velvet, under the direction of Mrs Trimmer and Mary Queen of Scots.

If this should meet the eye of the gentleman who favoured me with these disclosures, I trust he will excuse me for confessing that the sight of the rising sun, and the contemplation of the magnificent order of the vast universe, made me impatient of them. In a word, I was so impatient of them, that I was mightily glad to get out at the next station, and to exchange these clouds and vapours for the free air of heaven.

By that time it was a beautiful morning. As I walked away among such leaves as had already fallen from the golden, brown and russet trees, and as I looked around me on the wonders of Creation, and thought of the steady, unchanging and harmonious laws by which they are sustained, the gentleman's spiritual intercourse seemed to me as poor a piece of journey-work as ever this world saw. In which heathen state of mind, I came within view of the house, and stopped to examine it attentively.

It was a solitary house, standing in a sadly neglected garden: a pretty even square of some two acres. It was a house of about the time of George II; as stiff, as cold, as formal, and in as bad taste, as could possibly be desired by the most loyal admirer of the whole quartet of Georges. It was uninhabited, but had, within a year or two, been cheaply

5

repaired to render it habitable; I say cheaply, because the work had been done in a surface manner, and was already decaying as to the paint and plaster, though the colours were fresh. A lopsided board drooped over the garden wall, announcing that it was "to let on very reasonable terms, well furnished". It was much too closely and heavily shadowed by trees, and, in particular, there were six tall poplars before the front windows, which were excessively melancholy, and the site of which had been extremely ill chosen.

It was easy to see that it was an avoided house – a house that was shunned by the village, to which my eye was guided by a church spire some half a mile off – a house that nobody would take. And the natural inference was that it had the reputation of being a haunted house.

No period within the four-and-twenty hours of day and night is so solemn to me as the early morning. In the summertime, I often rise very early, and I am always on those occasions deeply impressed by the stillness and solitude around me. Besides that there is something awful in the being surrounded by familiar faces asleep – in the knowledge that those who are dearest to us, and to whom we are dearest, are profoundly unconscious of us, in an impassive state anticipative of that mysterious condition to which we are all tending – the stopped life, the broken threads of yesterday, the deserted seat, the closed book, the unfinished but abandoned occupation, all are images of death. The tranquillity of the hour is the tranquillity of death. The colour and the chill have the same association. Even a certain air that familiar household objects take upon them when they first emerge from the shadows of the night into the morning, of being newer, and as they used to be long ago, has its counterpart in the subsidence of the worn face of maturity or age, in death, into the old youthful look. Moreover, I once saw the apparition of my father at this hour. He was alive and well, and nothing ever came of it, but I saw him in the daylight, sitting with his back towards me, on a seat that stood beside my bed. His head was resting on his hand, and whether he was slumbering or grieving, I could not discern. Amazed to see him there, I sat up, moved my position, leant out of bed and watched him. As he did not move, I spoke to him more than once. As he did not move then, I became alarmed and laid my hand upon his shoulder, as I thought – and there was no such thing.

For all these reasons, and for others less easily and briefly stateable, I find the early morning to be my most ghostly time. Any house would be more or less haunted, to me, in the early morning, and a haunted house could scarcely address me to greater advantage than then.

I walked on into the village, with the desertion of this house upon my mind, and I found the landlord of the little inn sanding his doorstep. I bespoke breakfast, and broached the subject of the house.

"Is it haunted?" I asked.

The landlord looked at me, shook his head and answered, "I say nothing."

"Then it *is* haunted?"

"Well!" cried the landlord, in an outburst of frankness that had the appearance of desperation. "I wouldn't sleep in it."

"Why not?"

"If I wanted to have all the bells in a house ring, with nobody to ring 'em, and all the doors in a house bang with nobody to bang 'em, and all sorts of feet treading about with no feet there, why then," said the landlord, "I'd sleep in that house."

"Is anything seen there?"

The landlord looked at me again, and then, with his former appearance of desperation, called down his stable-yard or "Ikey!"

The call produced a high-shouldered young fellow, with a round red face, a short crop of sandy hair, a very broad humorous mouth, a turned-up nose and a great sleeved waistcoat of purple bars with mother-of-pearl buttons, that seemed to be growing upon him, and to be in a fair way – if it were not pruned – of covering his head and overrunning his boots.

"This gentleman wants to know," said the landlord, "if anything's seen at The Poplars."

"'Ooded woman with a howl," said Ikey, in a state of great freshness.

"Do you mean a cry?"

"I mean a bird, sir."

"A hooded woman with an owl. Dear me! Did you ever see her?"

"I seen the howl."

"Never the woman?"

"Not so plain as the howl, but they always keeps together."

"Has anybody ever seen the woman as plainly as the owl?"

"Lord bless you, sir! Lots."

"Who?"

"Lord bless you, sir! Lots."

"The general-dealer opposite, for instance, who is opening his shop?"

"Perkins? Bless you, Perkins wouldn't go a-nigh the place. No!" observed the young man, with considerable feeling. "He an't otherwise, an't Perkins, but an't such a fool as *that*."

(Here, the landlord murmured his confidence in Perkins's knowing better.)

"Who is – or who was – the hooded woman with the owl? Do you know?"

"Well!" said Ikey, holding up his cap with one hand while he scratched his head with the other. "They say, in general, that she was murdered, and the howl he 'ooted the while."

This very concise summary of the facts was all I could learn, except that a young man, as hearty and likely a young man as ever I see, had been took with fits and held down in 'em, after seeing the hooded woman. Also, that a personage dimly described as "a hold chap, a sort of a one-eyed tramp, answering to the name of Joby, unless you challenged him as Greenwood, and then he said, 'Why not? And even if so, mind your own business,'" had encountered the hooded woman a matter of five or six times. But I was not materially assisted by these witnesses; inasmuch as the first was in California, and the last was, as Ikey said (and he was confirmed by the landlord), "Anywheres".

Now, although I regard with a hushed and solemn fear the mysteries between which and this state of existence is interposed the barrier of the great trial and change that fall on all the things that live, and although I have not the audacity to pretend that I know anything of them, I can no more reconcile the mere banging of doors, ringing of bells, creaking of boards and suchlike insignificances, with all the majestic beauty and pervading analogy of all the divine rules that I am permitted to understand, than I had been able, a little while before, to yoke the spiritual intercourse of my fellow traveller to the chariot of the rising sun. Moreover, I had lived in two haunted houses – both abroad. In one of these, an old Italian palace, which bore the reputation of being very badly haunted indeed, and which had recently been twice abandoned on that account, I lived eight months, most tranquilly and pleasantly: notwithstanding that the house had a score of mysterious bedrooms, which were never used, and possessed, in one large room in which I sat reading, times out of number at all hours, and next to which I slept, a haunted chamber of the first pretensions. I gently hinted these considerations to the landlord. And as to this particular house having a bad name, I reasoned with him, why, how many things had bad names undeservedly, and how easy it was to give bad names, and did he not think that if he and I were persistently to whisper in the village that any weird-looking old drunken tinker of the neighbourhood had sold himself to the Devil, he would come in time to be suspected of that commercial venture! All this wise talk was perfectly ineffective with the landlord, I am bound to confess, and was as dead a failure as ever I made in my life.

To cut this part of the story short, I was piqued about the haunted house, and was already half resolved to take it. So, after breakfast, I got the keys from Perkins's brother-in-law (a whip and harness maker, who keeps the post office, and is under submission to a most rigorous wife of the Doubly Seceding Little Emmanuel persuasion) and went up to the house, attended by my landlord and by Ikey.

Within, I found it, as I had expected, transcendently dismal. The slowly changing shadows, waved on it from the heavy trees, were doleful in the last degree; the house was ill-placed, ill-built, ill-planned and ill-fitted. It was damp, it was not free from dry rot, there was a flavour of rats in it, and it was the gloomy victim of that indescribable decay which settles on all the work of man's hands whenever it is not turned to man's account. The kitchens and offices were too large and too remote from each other. Above stairs and below, waste tracks of passage intervened between patches of fertility represented by rooms, and there was a mouldy old well with a green growth upon it, hiding, like a murderous trap, near the bottom of the back stairs, under the double row of bells. One of these bells was labelled, on a black ground in faded white letters, MASTER B. This, they told me, was the bell that rang most.

"Who was Master B.?" I asked. "Is it known what he did while the owl hooted?"

"Rang the bell," said Ikey.

I was rather struck by the prompt dexterity with which this young man pitched his fur cap at the bell, and rang it himself. It was a loud, unpleasant bell, and made a very disagreeable sound. The other bells were inscribed, according to the names of the rooms to which their wires were conducted, as "Picture Room", "Double Room", "Clock Room" and the like. Following Master B.'s bell to its source, I found that young gentleman to have had but indifferent third-class accommodation in a triangular cabin under the cock-loft, with a corner fireplace which Master B. must have been exceedingly small if he were ever able to warm himself at, and a corner chimney piece like a pyramidal staircase to the ceiling for Tom Thumb. The papering of one side of the room had dropped down bodily, with fragments of plaster adhering to it, and almost blocked up the door. It appeared that Master B., in his spiritual condition, always made a point of pulling the paper down. Neither the landlord nor Ikey could suggest why he made such a fool of himself.

9

Except that the house had an immensely large rambling loft at top, I made no other discoveries. It was modestly well furnished, but sparely. Some of the furniture – say, a third – was as old as the house; the rest was of various periods within the last half century. I was referred to a corn-chandler in the marketplace of the country town to treat for the house. I went that day, and I took it for six months.

It was just the middle of October when I moved in with my maiden sister (I venture to call her eight-and-thirty, she is so very, very handsome, sensible and engaging). We took with us a deaf stable-man, my blood-hound Turk, two woman servants and a young person called an Odd Girl. I have reason to record of the attendant last enumerated, who was one of Saint Lawrence's Union Female Orphans, that she was a fatal mistake and a disastrous engagement.

The year was dying early, the leaves were falling fast, it was a raw cold day when we took possession, and the gloom of the house was most depressing. The cook (an amiable woman, but of a weak turn of intellect) burst into tears on beholding the kitchen, and requested that her silver watch might be delivered over to her sister (2 Tuppintock's Gardens, Ligg's Walk, Clapham Rise), in the event of anything happening to her from the damp. Streaker, the housemaid, feigned cheerfulness, but was the greater martyr. The Odd Girl, who had never been in the country, alone was pleased, and made arrangements for sowing an acorn in the garden outside the scullery window, and rearing an oak.

We went, before dark, through all the natural – as opposed to super-natural – miseries incidental to our state. Dispiriting reports ascended (like the smoke) from the basement in volumes, and descended from the upper rooms. There was no rolling pin, there was no salamander (which failed to surprise me, for I don't know what it is), there was nothing in the house; what there was, was broken, the last people must have lived like pigs, what could the meaning of the landlord be? Through these distresses, the Odd Girl was cheerful and exemplary. But within four hours after dark we had got into a supernatural groove, and the Odd Girl had seen "Eyes", and was in hysterics.

My sister and I had agreed to keep the haunting strictly to ourselves, and my impression was, and still is, that I had not left Ikey, when he helped to unload the cart, alone with the women, or any one of them, for one minute. Nevertheless, as I say, the Odd Girl had "seen Eyes" (no other explanation could ever be drawn from her) before nine, and by ten o'clock had had as much vinegar applied to her as would pickle a handsome salmon.

I leave a discerning public to judge of my feelings, when, under these untoward circumstances, at about half-past ten o'clock Master B.'s bell began to ring in a most infuriated manner, and Turk howled until the house resounded with his lamentations!

I hope I may never again be in a state of mind so unchristian as the mental frame in which I lived for some weeks, respecting the memory of Master B. Whether his bell was rung by rats, or mice, or bats, or wind, or what other accidental vibration, or sometimes by one cause, sometimes another and sometimes by collusion, I don't know, but certain it is that it did ring, two nights out of three, until I conceived the happy idea of twisting Master B.'s neck – in other words, breaking his bell short off – and silencing that young gentleman, as to my experience and belief, for ever.

But by that time, the Odd Girl had developed such improving powers of catalepsy that she had become a shining example of that very inconvenient disorder. She would stiffen like a Guy Fawkes endowed with unreason, on the most irrelevant occasions. I would address the servants in a lucid manner, pointing out to them that I had painted Master B.'s room and balked the paper, and taken Master B.'s bell away and balked the ringing, and if they could suppose that that confounded boy had lived and died, to clothe himself with no better behaviour than would most unquestionably have brought him and the sharpest particles of a birch broom into close acquaintance in the present imperfect state of existence, could they also suppose a mere poor human being, such as I was, capable by those contemptible means of counteracting and limiting the powers of the disembodied spirits of the dead, or of any spirits? I say I would become emphatic and cogent, not to say rather complacent, in such an address, when it would all go for nothing by reason of the Odd Girl's suddenly stiffening from the toes upwards, and glaring among us like a parochial petrifaction.

Streaker, the housemaid, too, had an attribute of a most discomfiting nature. I am unable to say whether she was of an unusually lymphatic temperament, or what else was the matter with her, but this young woman became a mere distillery for the production of the largest and most transparent tears I ever met with. Combined with these characteristics was a peculiar tenacity of hold in those specimens, so that they didn't fall, but hung upon her face and nose. In this condition, and mildly and deploringly shaking her head, her silence would throw me more heavily than the Admirable Crichton* could have done in a verbal disputation for a purse of money. Cook, likewise, always covered me with confusion as with a garment, by neatly winding up the session with the protest that the 'ouse was wearing her out, and by meekly repeating her last wishes regarding her silver watch.

As to our nightly life, the contagion of suspicion and fear was among us, and there is no such contagion under the sky. Hooded woman? According to the accounts, we were in a perfect convent of hooded women. Noises? With that contagion downstairs, I myself have sat in the dismal parlour, listening, until I have heard so many and such strange noises, that they would have chilled my blood if I had not warmed it by dashing out to make discoveries. Try this in bed, in the dead of night; try this at your own comfortable fireside, in the life of the night. You can fill any house with noises, if you will, until you have a noise for every nerve in your nervous system.

I repeat: the contagion of suspicion and fear was among us, and there is no such contagion under the sky. The women (their noses in a chronic state of excoriation from smelling salts), were always primed and loaded for a swoon, and ready to go off with hair-triggers. The two elder detached the Odd Girl on all expeditions that were considered doubly hazardous, and she always established the reputation of such adventures by coming back cataleptic. If Cook or Streaker went overhead after dark, we knew we should presently hear a bump on the ceiling, and this took place so constantly that it was as if a fighting man were engaged to go about the house, administering a touch of his art which I believe is called The Auctioneer to every domestic he met with.

It was in vain to do anything. It was in vain to be frightened, for the moment in one's own person, by a real owl, and then to show the owl. It was in vain to discover, by striking an accidental discord on the piano, that Turk always howled at particular notes and combinations. It was in vain to be a Rhadamanthus* with the bells, and if an unfortunate bell rang without leave, to have it down inexorably and silence it. It was in vain to fire up chimneys, let torches down the well, charge furiously into suspected rooms and recesses. We changed servants, and it was no better. The new set ran away, and a third set came, and it was no better. At last, our comfortable housekeeping got to be so disorganised and wretched that I one night dejectedly said to my sister:

"Patty, I begin to despair of our getting people to go on with us here, and I think we must give this up."

My sister, who is a woman of immense spirit, replied, "No, John, don't give it up. Don't be beaten, John. There is another way."

"And what is that?" said I.

"John," returned my sister, "if we are not to be driven out of this house, and that for no reason whatever that is apparent to you or me, we must help ourselves and take the house wholly and solely into our own hands."

"But the servants..." said I.

"Have no servants," said my sister boldly.

Like most people in my grade of life, I had never thought of the possibility of going on without those faithful obstructions. The notion was so new to me when suggested that I looked very doubtful.

"We know they come here to be frightened and infect one another, and we know they are frightened and do infect one another," said my sister.

"With the exception of Bottles," I observed, in a meditative tone.

(The deaf stableman. I kept him in my service, and still keep him, as a phenomenon of moroseness not to be matched in England.)

"To be sure, John," assented my sister, "except Bottles. And what does that go to prove? Bottles talks to nobody, and hears nobody unless he is absolutely roared at, and what alarm has Bottles ever given or taken! None."

This was perfectly true; the individual in question having retired, every night at ten o'clock, to his bed over the coach house, with no other company than a pitchfork and a pail of water. That the pail of water would have been over me, and the pitchfork through me, if I had put myself without announcement in Bottles's way after that minute, I had deposited in my own mind as a fact worth remembering. Neither had Bottles ever taken the least notice of any of our many uproars. An imperturbable and speechless man, he had sat at his supper, with Streaker present in a swoon, and the Odd Girl marble, and had only put another potato in his cheek, or profited by the general misery to help himself to beefsteak pie.

"And so," continued my sister, "I exempt Bottles. And considering, John, that the house is too large, and perhaps too lonely, to be kept well in hand by Bottles, you and me, I propose that we cast among our friends for a certain selected number of the most reliable and willing, form a society here for three months, wait upon ourselves and one another, live cheerfully and socially and see what happens."

I was so charmed with my sister that I embraced her on the spot, and went into the plan with the greatest ardour.

We were then in the third week of November, but we took our measures so vigorously, and were so well seconded by the friends in whom we confided, that there was still a week of the month unexpired when our party all came down together merrily, and mustered in the haunted house.

I will mention in this place two small changes that I made while my sister and I were yet alone. It occurring to me as not improbable that Turk howled in the house at night partly because he wanted to get out of it, I stationed him in his kennel outside, but unchained, and I seriously warned the village that any man who came in his way must not expect to leave without a rip in his own throat. I then casually asked Ikey if he were a judge of a gun. On his saying, "Yes, sir, I knows a good gun when I sees her," I begged the favour of his stepping up to the house and looking at mine.

"*She's* a true one, sir," said Ikey, after inspecting a double-barrelled rifle that I bought in New York a few years ago. "No mistake about *her*, sir."

"Ikey," said I, "don't mention it; I have seen something in this house."

"No, sir?" he whispered, greedily opening his eyes. "'Ooded lady, sir?"

"Don't be frightened," said I. "It was a figure rather like you."

"Lord, sir?"

"Ikey!" said I, shaking hands with him warmly – I may say affectionately – "if there is any truth in these ghost stories, the greatest service I can do you is to fire at that figure. And I promise you, by heaven and earth, I will do it with this gun if I see it again!"

The young man thanked me, and took his leave with some little precipitation, after declining a glass of liquor. I imparted my secret to him because I had never quite forgotten his throwing his cap at the bell; because I had, on another occasion, noticed something very like a fur cap, lying not far from the bell, one night when it had burst out ringing, and because I had remarked that we were at our ghostliest whenever he came up in the evening to comfort the servants. Let me do Ikey no injustice. He was afraid of the house, and believed in its being haunted, and yet he would play false on the haunting side, so surely as he got an opportunity. The Odd Girl's case was exactly similar. She went about the house in a state of real terror, and yet lied monstrously and wilfully, and invented many of the alarms she spread, and made many of the sounds we heard. I had had my eye on the two, and I know it. It is not necessary for me, here, to account for this preposterous state of mind; I content myself with remarking that it is familiarly known to every intelligent man who has had a fair medical, legal or other watchful experience; that it is as well established and as common a state of mind as any with which observers are acquainted, and that it is one of the first elements, above all others, rationally to be suspected in, and strictly looked for, and separated from, any question of this kind.

To return to our party. The first thing we did when we were all assembled was to draw lots for bedrooms. That done, and every bedroom, and indeed, the whole house, having been minutely examined by the whole body, we allotted the various household duties, as if we had been on a gypsy party, or a yachting party, or a hunting party, or were shipwrecked. I then recounted the floating rumours concerning the hooded lady, the owl and Master B., with others, still more filmy, which had floated about during our occupation, relative to some ridiculous old ghost of a round table, and also to an impalpable Jackass, whom nobody was ever able to catch. Some of these ideas I really believe our people below had communicated to one another in some diseased way without conveying them in words. We then gravely called one another to witness that we were not there to be deceived, or to deceive – which we considered pretty much the same thing – and that, with a serious sense of responsibility, we would be strictly true to one another, and would strictly follow out the truth. The understanding was established that anyone who heard unusual noises in the night, and who wished to trace them, should knock at my door; lastly, that on Twelfth Night, the last day of the holy Christmas, all our individual experiences since that then present hour of our coming together in the haunted house should be brought to light for the good of all, and that we would hold our peace on the subject till then, unless on some remarkable provocation to break silence.

We were in number and in character, as follows:

First – to get my sister and myself out of the way – there were we two. In the drawing of lots, my sister drew her own room, and I drew Master B.'s. Next there was our first cousin John Herschel, so called after the great astronomer – than whom, I suppose, a better man at a telescope does not breathe. With him was his wife: a charming creature to whom he had been married in the previous spring. I thought it (under the circumstances) rather imprudent to bring her, because there is no knowing what even a false alarm may do at such a time, but I suppose he knew his own business best, and I must say that if she had been *my* wife, I never could have left her endearing and bright face behind. They drew the Clock Room. Alfred Starling, an uncommonly agreeable young fellow of eight-and-twenty for whom I have the greatest liking, was in the Double Room: mine, usually, and designated by that name from having a dressing room within it, with two large and cumbersome windows which no wedges I was ever able to make would keep from shaking in any weather, wind or no wind. Alfred is a young fellow who pretends to be "fast" (another word for loose, as I understand the term), but who is much too good and sensible for that nonsense, and who would have distinguished himself before now if his father had not unfortunately left him a small independence of two hundred a year, on the strength of which his only occupation in life has been to spend six. I am in hopes, however, that his banker may break, or that he may enter into some speculation guaranteed to pay twenty per cent, for I am convinced that if he could only be ruined, his fortune is made. Belinda Bates, bosom friend of my sister, and a most intellectual, amiable and delightful girl, got the Picture Room. She has a fine genius for poetry, combined with real business earnestness, and "goes in" – to use an expression of Alfred's – for Woman's mission, Woman's rights, Woman's wrongs and everything that is Woman's with a capital W, or is not and ought to be. "Most praiseworthy, my dear, and Heaven prosper you!" I whispered to her on the first night of my taking leave of her at the Picture Room door. "But don't overdo it. And in respect of the great necessity there is, my darling, for more employments being within the reach of Woman than our civilization has as yet assigned to her, don't fly at the unfortunate men, even those men who are at first sight in your way, as if they were the natural oppressors of your sex; for, trust me, Belinda, they do sometimes spend their wages among wives and daughters, sisters, mothers, aunts and grandmothers, and the play is, really, not *all* Wolf and Red Riding Hood, but has other parts in it." However, I digress.

Belinda, as I have mentioned, occupied the Picture Room. We had but three other chambers: the Corner Room, the Cupboard Room and the Garden Room. My old friend, Jack Governor, "slung his hammock", as he called it, in the Corner Room. I have always regarded Jack as the finest-looking sailor that ever sailed. He is grey now, but as handsome as he was a quarter of a century ago – nay, handsomer. A portly, cheery, well-built figure of a broad-shouldered man, with a frank smile, a brilliant dark eye and a rich dark eyebrow. I remember those under darker hair, and they look all the better for the silver setting. He has been wherever his Union namesake flies, has Jack, and I have met old shipmates of his, away in the Mediterranean and on the other side of the Atlantic, who have beamed and brightened at the casual mention of his name, and have cried, "You know Jack Governor? Then you know a prince of men!" That he is! And so unmistakably a naval officer, that if you were to meet him coming out of an Eskimo snow hut in sealskin, you would be vaguely persuaded he was in full naval uniform.

Jack once had that bright clear eye of his on my sister, but it fell out that he married another lady and took her to South America, where she died. This was a dozen years ago or more. He brought down with him to our haunted house a little cask of salt beef, for he is always convinced that all salt beef not of his own pickling is mere carrion, and invariably, when he goes to London, packs a piece in his portmanteau. He had also volunteered to bring with him one "Nat Beaver", an old comrade of his, captain of a merchantman. Mr Beaver, with a thickset wooden face and figure, and apparently as hard as a block all over, proved to be an intelligent man, with a world of watery experiences in him, and great practical knowledge. At times, there was a curious nervousness about him, apparently the lingering result of some old illness, but it seldom lasted many minutes. He got the Cupboard Room, and lay there next to Mr Undery, my friend and solicitor, who came down, in an amateur capacity, "to go through with it", as he said, and who plays whist better than the whole Law List, from the red cover at the beginning to the red cover at the end.

I never was happier in my life, and I believe it was the universal feeling among us. Jack Governor, always a man of wonderful resources, was chief cook, and made some of the best dishes I ever ate, including unapproachable curries. My sister was pastry cook and confectioner. Starling and I were cook's mate, turn and turn about, and on special occasions the chief cook "pressed" Mr Beaver. We had a great deal of outdoor sport and exercise, but nothing was neglected within, and there was no ill humour or misunderstanding among us, and our evenings were so delightful that we had at least one good reason for being reluctant to go to bed.

We had a few night alarms in the beginning. On the first night, I was knocked up by Jack with a most wonderful ship's lantern in his hand, like the gills of some monster of the deep, who informed me that he was "going aloft to the main truck", to have the weathercock down. It was a stormy night and I remonstrated, but Jack called my attention to its making a sound like a cry of despair, and said somebody would be "hailing a ghost" presently, if it wasn't done. So, up to the top of the house, where I could hardly stand for the wind, we went, accompanied by Mr Beaver, and there Jack, lantern and all with Mr Beaver after him, swarmed up to the top of a cupola, some two dozen feet above the chimneys, and stood upon nothing particular, coolly knocking the weathercock off, until they both got into such good spirits with the wind and the height that I thought they would never come down. Another night, they turned out again, and had a chimney cowl off. Another night, they found something else. On several occasions, they both, in the coolest manner, simultaneously dropped out of their respective bedroom windows, hand over hand by their counterpanes, to "overhaul" something mysterious in the garden.

The engagement among us was faithfully kept, and nobody revealed anything. All we knew was, if anyone's room were haunted, no one looked the worse for it. Christmas came, and we had noble Christmas fare ("all hands" had been pressed for the pudding), and Twelfth Night came, and our store of mincemeat was ample to hold out to the last day of our time, and our cake was quite a glorious sight. It was then, as we all sat round the table and the fire, that I recited the terms of our compact, and called first for:

2

The Ghost in the Clock Room

by Hesba Stretton

M Y COUSIN, John Herschel, turned rather red, and turned rather white, and said he could not deny that his room had been haunted. The spirit of a woman had pervaded it. On being asked by several voices whether the spirit had taken any terrible or ugly shape, my cousin drew his wife's arm through his own, and said decidedly, "No." To the question, had his wife been aware of the spirit? he answered, "Yes." Had it spoken? "Oh dear, yes!" As to the question, "What did it say?" he replied apologetically that he could have wished his wife would have undertaken to answer, for she would have executed it much better than he. However, she had made him promise to be the mouthpiece of the spirit, and was very anxious that he should withhold nothing; so he would do his best, subject to her correction. "Suppose the spirit," added my cousin, as he finally prepared himself for beginning, "to be my wife here, sitting among us":

I was an orphan from my infancy, with six elder half-sisters. A long and persistent course of training imposed upon me the yoke of a second and diverse nature, and I grew up as much the child of my eldest sister, Barbara, as I was the daughter of my deceased parents.

Barbara, in all her private plans, as in all her domestic decrees, inexorably decided that her sisters must be married, and so powerful had been her single but inflexible will, that each of them had been advantageously settled, excepting myself, upon whom she built her highest hopes.

Most people know a character such as I had grown – a mindless, flirting girl, whose acknowledged vocation was the hunting and catching of an eligible match – rather pretty, lively and just sentimental enough to make me a very pleasant companion for an idle hour or two, as I exacted and enjoyed the slight attentions an unemployed man is pleased to offer. There was scarcely a young man in the neighbourhood with whom I had not coquetted. I had served my seven years' apprenticeship to my profession, and had passed my twenty-fifth birthday without having achieved my purpose, when Barbara's patience was wearied, and she spoke to me with a decision and explicitness we had always avoided, for, on some subjects, it is better to have a silent understanding than an expressed opinion.

"Stella," she said solemnly, "you are now five-and-twenty, and every one of your sisters were in homes of their own before they were your age; yet none of them had your advantages or your talents. But I must tell you frankly your chances are on the wane, and, unless you exert yourself, our plans must fail. I have observed an error into which you have fallen, and which I have not mentioned before. Besides your very open and indiscriminate flirtations – which young men regard only as an amusing pastime – you have a way with you of rallying and laughing at anyone who begins to look really serious. Now your opportunity rests upon the moment when they begin to be in earnest in their manner. Then you should seem confused and silenced; you ought to lose your vivacity, and half avoid them, seeming almost frightened and quite bewildered by the change. A little melancholy goes a deal further than the utmost cheerfulness, for, if a man believes you can live without him, he will not give you a second thought. I could name half a dozen most eligible settlements you have lost by laughing at the wrong minute. Mortify a man's self-love, Stella, and you can never heal the wound."

I paused for a minute or two before I answered, for the original suppressed nature that I had inherited from my unknown mother was stirring unwonted feeling in my heart.

"Barbara," I answered, with timidity, "among all the people I have known, I never saw one whom I could reverence and look up to; nor, I am half ashamed to use the word, whom I could love."

"I do not wonder you are ashamed," said Barbara severely. "At your age, you cannot expect to fall in love like a girl of seventeen. But I tell you, definitely and distinctly, it is necessary that you should marry, and we had better work in concert now. So, if you will decide upon anyone, I will give you every assistance in my power, and if you will only concentrate your wishes and abilities, you cannot fail. Propinquity is all you require, if you once make up your mind."

"I do not like anyone I know," I replied moodily, "and I have no chance with those who have known me; so I decide upon besieging Martin Fraser."

Barbara received this announcement with a snort of derisive anger.

The neighbourhood in which we lived was a populous iron district, where, though there were few families of ancient birth or high standing, there were many of our own station, forming a pleasant, hospitable social class. Our residences were commodious modern houses, built at convenient distances from each other. Some of these, including our own, were the property of an infirm old man, who dwelt in his family mansion, the last of the many gabled, half-timbered Elizabethan houses which had stood upon the undiscovered iron and coal fields. The last relics of the rural aristocracy of the district, Mr Fraser and his son led a strictly recluse life, avoiding all communications with their neighbours, whose gaiety and hospitality they could not reciprocate. No one intruded upon their privacy, excepting for the most necessary business transactions. The elder man was almost bedridden, and the younger was said to be entirely absorbed in scientific pursuits. No wonder that Barbara laughed, but her ridicule only excited and confirmed my determination, and the very difficulty of the enterprise gave it the interest that all my other efforts had lacked. I argued obstinately with Barbara till I won her consent.

"You must write to old Mr Fraser," I said. "Do not mention the young one, and say your youngest sister is studying astronomy, and, as he possesses the only telescope in the country, you will be greatly indebted to him if he would let her see it."

"There is one thing in your favour," Barbara remarked, as she sat down to write. "The old gentleman was once engaged to your mother."

Oh! I am humbled to think how shrewdly we managed our business, and extorted a kind invitation from Mr Fraser to the "daughter of his old friend, Maria Horley".

It was an evening in February when, accompanied only by an old servant – for Barbara was not included in the invitation – I first crossed the threshold of Martin Fraser's home.

An air of profound peace pervaded the dwelling. I entered it with a vague, uneasy consciousness of unfitness and treachery. My attendant remained in the entrance hall, and, as I was conducted to the library, a feeling of shyness stole over me, which was prompting me to retreat, but, with the recollection that I was becomingly dressed, I regained my confidence, and advanced smilingly into the room. It was a low, oaken-panelled room, sombre, with massive antique furniture that threw deep and curious shadows around, in the flickering light of a fire, by which stood, instead of the recluse Martin Fraser whom I expected to meet, a quaint little child, dressed in the garb of a woman, and with a woman's self-possession and ease of manner.

"I am very glad to see you. You are welcome," she said, advancing to meet me, and extending her hand to lead me to a seat. She clasped my hand with a firm and peculiar grasp – a clasp of guidance and assistance, quite unlike the ordinary timidity or inertness of a child's manner, and, placing me in a chair beside the fire, she seated herself nearly opposite me.

I made a few embarrassed remarks, to which she replied, and then I noticed her furtively and in silence. A huge black retriever lay motionless at her feet, which rested upon him, covered with the folds of the long robe-like dress she wore. There was an expression of placidity, slightly pensive, upon her tiny features, heightened by a peculiar habit of closing the eyes, which is rarely seen in children, and always gives them a statuesque appearance. It seemed as though she had withdrawn herself into a solitary self-communing, of which there could be no expression either by words or looks. I grew afraid of the silent, weird-like creature, sitting without apparent breath or motion in the dancing firelight, and I was glad when the door opened, and the object of my pursuit entered. I looked at him inquisitively, for I had recovered from my sense of treachery, and it amused me to think how unconscious he was of our definite plans concerning him. Hitherto the young men I had met had a fear of being caught greater than my desire to catch them, so our contest had been an open and equal one, but Martin Fraser knew nothing of the wiles of woman. I remembered that my dark-blue eyes were considered expressive, when I looked up to meet his gaze, but when he accosted me with an air of grave preoccupation and of courteous indifference that would not permit him to notice my personal charms, I trembled to think that all I knew of astronomy was what I had learnt at school in Magnall's *Questions*.*

The grave, austere man said at once:

"My father, Mr Fraser, is altogether confined to his own rooms, but he desires the favour of a visit from you. Upon me develops the honour of showing you what you require to view through the telescope, and, while I adjust it, will you oblige him by conversing with him for a few minutes? Lucy Fraser will accompany you."

The child rose and, taking my hand again in her firm hold, led me to the old man's sitting room.

"You are like your mother, child," he said, after looking at me long, "you have her face and eyes; not a whit like your sister Barbara. How did you come by your out-of-the-way name, Stella?"

"My father named me after a favourite racer," I answered, for the first time giving the simple derivation of my name.

"Just like him," laughed the old man, "I remember the horse well. I knew your father as well as I do my son Martin. You have seen my son, young lady? Yes, I thought so, and this is my granddaughter, Lucy Fraser, the last chip of the old block, for my son is not a marrying man, and we have adopted her as our heir, and she is always to keep her name, and be the founder of another line of Frasers."

The child stood with pensive, downcast eyes, as though already bowed down by her weight of cares and responsibilities; the old man chatted on, till the deep tones of an organ resounded through the house.

"My uncle is ready for us," she said to me.

We paused at the library door, for I laid my hand restrainingly on Lucy Fraser's shoulder, and stood listening to the wonderful music the organ poured forth. It was such as I had never heard before, roaring and swelling like the ceaseless surging of the sea, and, here and there, a single wailing note which seemed to pierce me with an inexpressible pain. When it had ended, I stood before Martin Fraser silent and subdued.

The telescope had been carried out to the end of the terrace, where the house could not intercept our view, and thither Lucy Fraser and I followed the astronomer. We stood upon the highest perceptible point of an imperceptibly rising tableland, the horizon of which was from twenty to forty miles distant. An infinite dome of sky was expanded above us, an ocean of firmament of which the dwellers among houses and mountains can have but little conception. The troops of glittering stars, the dark, shrouding night, the unaccustomed voices of my companions, deepened the awe that oppressed me, and, as I stood between them, I became as earnest and occupied as themselves. I forgot everything but the incomprehensible grandeur of the universe revealed to me, and the majestic sweep of the planets across the field of the telescope. What a freshness of awe and delight came over me! What floods of thought came, wave upon wave, across my mind! And how insignificant I felt before this wilderness of worlds!

I asked, with the humility of a child – for all affectation had been charmed away – if I might come again soon?

Martin Fraser met my uplifted eyes with a keen and penetrating look. I did not quail under it, for I was thinking only of the stars. As he looked, his mouth relaxed into a pleased and genial smile.

"We shall always be glad to see you," he replied.

Barbara was sitting up for me when I returned, and was about to address me with some worldly speculative remark, when I interrupted her quickly. "Not one word, Barbara, not one question, or I never go near the Holmes again."

I cannot dwell upon details. I went often to the house. Into the dull routine of Mr Fraser and Lucy's life, I came (I suppose) like a streak of sunshine, lighting up the cloud that had been creeping over them. To both, I brought wholesome excitement and merriment, and so I became dear and necessary to them. But over myself, there came a great and an almost incredible change. I had been frivolous, self-seeking, soulless, but the solemn study I had begun, with other studies that came in its train, awoke me from my inanity to a life of mental activity. I absolutely forgot my purpose, for I had at once perceived that Martin Fraser was as distant and as self-poised as the Polar Star. So I became to him merely a diligent and insatiable pupil, and he was to me only a grave and exacting master, to be propitiated by my most profound reverence. Each time I crossed the threshold of his quiet home, all the worldliness and coquetry of my nature fell from my soul like an unfit garment, and I entered as into a temple, simple, real and worshipping.

The happy summer passed away, the autumn crept on, and for eight months I had visited the Frasers constantly, and had never, by word, or look, or tone, intentionally deceived them.

Lucy Fraser and I had long looked forward to an eclipse of the moon, which was visible early in October. I left my home alone in the twilight of that evening, my thoughts dwelling upon the coming pleasure, when, just as I drew near the Holmes, there overtook me one of the young men with whom I had flirted in former times.

"Good evening, Stella," he exclaimed familiarly, "I have not seen you for a long time. Ah! you are pursuing other game I suppose, but are you not aiming rather too high this time? Well, you are in luck just now, for if Martin Fraser does not come forwards, there is George Yorke, just come home from Australia with an immense fortune, and he is longing to remind you of some tender passages between you before he went out. He was showing us a lock of your hair after dinner at the Crown yesterday."

I listened to this speech with no outward demonstration, but the reality and mortification of my degradation was gnawing me, and, hastening onwards to my sanctuary, I sought the presence of my little Lucy Fraser.

"I have done wrong today," she said. "I have been deceitful. I think I ought to tell you that you may not think too well of me, but I want you to love me as much as ever. I have not told a story, but I have acted one."

Lucy Fraser leant her tiny brow upon her tiny fingers, and her eyes closed in silent self-reading.

"My uncle says," she continued, looking up for a moment, and blushing like a woman, "that women are, perhaps, less truthful than men. Because they cannot do things by strength, they do them by cunning. They live falsely. They deceive their own selves. Sometimes women deceive for amusement. He has taught me some words which I shall understand better some day:

> To thine own self be true,
> And it will follow as the night the day,
> Thou canst not then be false to any man."

I stood before the child abashed and speechless, listening with burning cheeks.

"Grandpa showed me a verse in the Bible which is awful to me. Listen. 'I find more bitter than death the woman whose heart is snares and nets, and her hands as bands: whoso pleaseth God shall escape from her, but the sinner shall be taken by her.'"

I hid my face in my hands though no eye was on me, for Lucy Fraser had veiled hers with their tremulous lids, and as I stood confounded and self-accused, a hand was laid upon my arm, and Martin Fraser's voice said, "The eclipse, Stella!"

I started at his first utterance of my name, which he had never spoken before. I was completely unnerved when I found that Lucy Fraser was not to accompany us on the terrace. As Martin Fraser stooped to see if the telescope were rightly adjusted for my use, I shrank from him.

"What is the meaning of this, Stella?" he exclaimed, as I burst into tears. "Shall I speak to you now, Stella?" he said. "While there is yet time, before you leave us. Does your heart cling to us as our hearts cling to you, till we dare not think of the void there will be in our home when you are gone? We did not live before we knew you. You are our health and our life. I have noted you as I never watched a woman before, and I find no fault in you, my pearl, my jewel, my star. Hitherto, woman and deceit have been inseparably conjoined in my mind, but your innocent heart is the home of truth. I know you have had no thought of this, and my vehemence alarms you, but tell me plainly if you can love me?"

He had taken me in his arms, and my head rested against his strongly throbbing heart. His sternness and austerity were gone, and he offered me the undiminished wealth of a love that had not been wasted in fickle likings. My success was perfect, and how gladly would I have remained there till my silence had grown eloquent! But Barbara rose to my memory, and Lucy Fraser's words still tingled in my ears. The black shadow eating away the heart of the moon seemed to pause in its measured motion. All heaven looked down upon us through the solemn stars. The rustling leaves were hushed, and the scented autumn breeze ceased for a minute; a cloud of truth-compelling witnesses echoed the cry of my awakened conscience. I withdrew myself, sad and shame-stricken.

"Martin Fraser," I said, "your words constrain me to be true. I am the falsest woman you ever met. I came here with the sole and definite intention of attracting you, and if you had ever gone out into our circle, you would have heard of me only as a flirt, a heartless coquette. I dare not bring my falsehood to your fireside, and the bitterness of death to your heart. Do not speak to me now; have patience, and I will write to you!"

He would have detained me, but I sprang away and, running swiftly down the avenue, I passed out of my Eden, with the sentence of perpetual banishment in my heart. The eclipse was at the full, and a horror of darkness and dismay engulfed me as I stood shivering and sobbing under the restless poplars.

Barbara met me as I hastened to hide myself in my own room and, with her cold glittering eyes fixed enquiringly on me, said:

"Well, what is the matter with you?"

"Nothing," I answered, "only I am tired of astronomy, and I shall not go to the Holmes again. It is of no use."

"I always said so," she replied. "However, to bring matters to a crisis, I gave Mr Fraser notice we should leave at Christmas. Then you are satisfied that it would be a waste of time to continue going there?"

"Quite," I said, and passed on to my room, to learn, through the weary hours of that night, what desolation and hopelessness meant.

The next day I wrote to Martin Fraser, in every word sacred truth, excepting that, self-deceived, and with a false pride even in my utter humiliation, I told him I had not loved, and did not love him.

The first object upon which my eyes rested every joyless morning were the tall poplar trees, waving round his house, and beckoning maddeningly to me. The last thing I saw at night was the steady light in his library, shining like a star among the laurels. But him I could never see, for my letter had been too explicit to suggest a hope, and I could not, for shame, attempt to meet him in his walks. All that remained for me was to return to my former life, if I could by any means feed my hungering and fainting soul with the husks that had once satisfied me.

George Yorke renewed his addresses to me, offering me wealth beyond our expectations. It was a sore temptation, for before me lay a monotonous and fretted life with Barbara, and a solitary, uncared-for old age. Why could I not live as thousands of other women, who were not unhappy wives? But I remembered a passage I had read in one of Martin's books: "It is not always our duty to marry, but it is always our duty to side by right, not to purchase happiness by loss of honour, not to avoid unweddedness by untruthfulness", and, setting my face steadily to meet the bleakness and bareness of my lot, I rejected the proposal.

Barbara was terribly exasperated, and very miserable we both were, until she accepted an invitation to spend the Christmas with one of her sisters, while I was left, with my old nurse, to superintend the moving of the furniture. I wished to linger in our old home till the last moment, and I was glad to be alone on Christmas Day in the deserted house, that, in solitude, I might make my mental record of all its associations and remembrances, before the place knew me no more. So, on Christmas Eve, I wandered through the empty rooms – not more empty than my heart – which was being dismantled of its memories and newer but deeper tendernesses, until I paused mechanically before the window, whence I had often looked across to the Holmes.

The air had been dense and murky all day, with thickly falling snow, but the storm was over, and the moonless sky bright with stars, while the glistening snow reflected light enough to show me where stood, like a dark mass against the sky, the house of Martin Fraser. His room was dark, as it had been for many nights before, but old Mr Fraser's window, which was nearer to our house, emitted a brilliant light across the white lawn. I was exhausted with overwork and over-excitement, and leaning there, pressing my heated cheeks against the frosty panes, I rehearsed to myself all the incidents of my intercourse with them, and there followed through my mind picture after picture, dream within dream, visions of the happiness that might have been mine.

As I stood thus, with tears stealing through the clasped hands that covered my eyes, my nurse came in to close the shutters. She started nervously when she saw me.

"I thought you were your mother," she exclaimed. "I have seen her stand just so, hundreds of times."

"Susan, how was it that my mother did not marry Mr Fraser?"

"They were like other people – didn't understand one another, much as they were in love," she answered. "Mr Fraser's first marriage had been for money, and was not a happy one, so he had grown something stern.

27

They quarrelled, and your mother was provoked to marry Mr Gretton, your father. Well! Mr Fraser became an old man all at once, and scarcely ever left his own house; so that she never saw him again, near as he lived – though I have often seen her, when your father was off to balls or races or public meetings, standing here, just as you stood now. Only the last time you were in her arms, she was leaning against this window when I brought you in to say goodnight, and she whispered softly, looking up to heaven, 'I have tried to do my duty to my husband and to my little child!'"

"Nurse," I said, "leave me; do not shut the window yet." It was no longer a selfish emotion that possessed me. I had been murmuring that there was no sorrow like my sorrow, but my mother's error had been graver, and her trials deeper than mine. The burden she had borne had weighed her down into an early grave, but it had not passed away from earth with her. It rested now, heavily augmented by her death, upon the heart of an aged man, who, doubtless, in the contemplative time, was reviewing the events of his past life, and this, chiefly, because it was the saddest of them all. I longed to see him once again – to see him who had mourned my mother's death more bitterly and lastingly than any other being, and I determined to steal secretly across the fields and up the avenue, and, if his window were uncurtained, as its brightness suggested, to look upon him once more in remembrance of my mother.

I hesitated upon our doorstep, as though my mother and myself were both concerned in some doubtful enterprise, but, with the hardihood of my nature, I drove away the scruple and passed on into the frosty night.

Yes, the window was uncurtained. I could tell that at the avenue gate, and I should see him, whom my mother loved, lying alone and uncheered upon his couch, as he would lie now all his weary years through, till Lucy Fraser was old enough to be a daughter to him. And then I remembered a rumour that the old man's grandchild was dying, which Susan had told me sorrowfully an hour or two ago, and, growing bewildered, I ran on swiftly until I stood before the window.

It was no longer an invalid's room; the couch was gone and the sheltering screen, and Lucy's little chair within it. Neither were there any appliances of modern luxury or wealth; no softness, nor colouring, nor gorgeousness – it was simply the library and workroom of a busy student, who was forgetful and negligent of comfort. Yet, such as it was, my heart recognized it as home. There Martin sat, deep, as was his wont, in complicated calculations, and frequent reference to the books that were strewn about.

Could it be possible that yonder absorbed man had once spoken to me passionately of love, and now he sat in light and warmth, and indifference, almost within reach of my hand, while I, like an outcast, stood in cold, and darkness, and despair? Was there, then, no echo of my footstep lingering about the threshold, and no shadowy memory of my face coming between him and his studies? I had forfeited the right to sit beside him, reading the observations his pencil noted down, and chasing away the gloom that was deepening on his nature, and I had not the hope, which would have been really hope and a consolation to me, that some other woman, more true and more worthy, would by and by own my forfeited right.

I heard a bell tinkle, and Martin rose and left the room. I wondered if I should have time to creep in, and steal but one scrap of paper which had been thrown aside carelessly, but, as I tremblingly held the handle of the glass door, he returned, bearing in his arms the emaciated form of little Lucy Fraser. He had wrapped her carefully in a large cloak, and now, as he wheeled a chair to the fire and placed her in it, every rigid lineament of his countenance was softened into tenderness. I stretched out my arms towards him with an intense yearning to be gathered again to his noble heart, and have this chill and darkness dissipated; I turned away, with this last tender image of him graven on my memory, to retrace my steps to my desolate home.

There was a sudden twittering in the ivy overhead, and a little bird, pushed out of its nest into the cold night air, came fluttering down, and flew against the lit panes. In an instant, his dog, which had been uneasy at my vicinity before, stood baying at the window, and I had only time to escape and hide myself among the shrubs, when he opened it, and stepped out upon the terrace. The dog tracked down the path by which I had come, barking joyfully as he careered along the open fields, and, as Martin looked round, I cowered more closely into the deepest shadows. I knew he must find me, for my footmarks were plain upon the newly fallen snow, and an extravagant sensation of shame and gladness overpowered me. I saw him lose the footprints once or twice, but at last he was upon the right trace, and, lifting the boughs beneath which I had hidden, he found me among the laurels. I was crouching, and he stooped down curiously.

"It is Stella," I said faintly.

"Stella?" he echoed.

He lifted me from the ground like a truant child, whom he had expected home every hour, carried me across the terrace into the library, and set me down in the light and warmth of his own hearth. One little kiss to the child, whose eyes beamed with a strange light upon us, and then, taking both my hands in his, he bent down and read my face. I met his gaze unshrinkingly, eye to eye. We sounded the depths of each other's heart in that long, unwavering look. Never more could there be doubt or mistrust; never again deception or misconstruction between us.

Our star had arisen, and full orbed, rounded into perfection, shed a soft and brilliant light upon the years to come. Chime after chime, like the marriage peal of our souls, came the sound of distant bells across the snow, and roused us from our reverie.

"I thought I had lost you altogether," said Martin to me. "I believed you would come back to me, somehow, at some time, but this evening I heard that you were gone, and I was telling Lucy Fraser so, not long since. She has been pining to see you."

Now he suffered me to take the child upon my lap, and she nestled close to me, with a weary sigh, resting her head upon my bosom. Just then, we heard the carol singers coming up the avenue, and Martin drew the curtains over the window, before which they stationed themselves to sing the legend of the miraculous star in the East.

When the singers ended and raised their cry of "We wish you a merry Christmas, and a happy New Year!" he went out into the porch to speak to them, and I hid my face in the child's curls, and thanked God who had so changed me.

"But what is this, Martin?" I cried in terror, as I raised my head, on his return.

The child's downcast eyes were closely sealed, and her little firm hand had grown lax and nerveless. Insensible and breathless, she lay in my arms like a withering flower.

"It is only fainting," said Martin, "she has been drooping ever since you left us, Stella, and my only hope of her recovery rests in your ministering care."

All that night, I sat with the little child resting on my bosom, revived from her death-like swoon, and sleeping calmly in my arms because she was already beginning to share in the life and joy and brightness of my heart. There was perfect silence and tranquillity enclosing us in a blissful oasis, interrupted only once by the entrance of my nurse, who had been found by Martin in a state of the utmost perplexity and alarm.

The happy Christmas morning dawned. I asked my nurse to arrange my hair in the style in which my mother used to wear hers. And when, after a long conversation with Susan, Mr Fraser received me as his daughter with great emotion and affection, and oftener called me Maria than Stella, I was satisfied to be identified with my mother. Then, in the evening, sitting amongst them, a passion of trembling and weeping seized me, which could only be soothed by their fondest assurances. After which I sang them some old songs, with nothing in them but their simple melody, and Mr Fraser talked freely of former years and of the times to come, and Lucy's eyes almost laughed.

Then Martin took me home along the familiar path, which I had so often traversed alone and fearless, but the excess of gladness made me timid, and at every unusual sound I crept closer to him, with a sweet sense of being protected.

One sunny day in spring, with blithe Lucy and triumphant dictatress Barbara for my bridesmaids, I accepted, humbly and joyfully, the lot of being Martin Fraser's wife. And even in the scenes of the empty-headed folly of my girlhood, I thenceforth tried to be better, and to do my duty in love, gratitude and devotion. Only, at first, Martin pretended not to believe that on that night I stole out to have a last glimpse, not of him, but of his father, I knowing nothing of the change that had transformed Mr Fraser's sitting room into his own study.

3

The Ghost in the Double Room

by George Augustus Sala

W AS THE NEXT GHOST on my list. I had noted the rooms down in the order in which they were drawn, and this was the order we were to follow. I invoked the spectre of the Double Room, with the least possible delay, because we all observed John Herschel's wife to be much affected, and we all refrained, as if by common consent, from glancing at one another. Alfred Starling, with the tact and good feeling which are never wanting in him, briskly responded to my call, and declared the Double Room to be haunted by the Ghost of the Ague.

"What is the Ghost of the Ague like?" asked everyone, when there had been a laugh.

"Like?" said Alfred. "Like the Ague."

"What is the Ague like?" asked somebody.

"Don't you know?" said Alfred. "I'll tell you."

We had both, Tilly – by which affectionate diminutive I mean my adored Matilda – and your humble servant, agreed that it was not only expedient, but in the highest degree contrary to the duty we owed to the community at large, to wait any longer. I had a hundred arguments to bring forwards against the baleful effects of long engagements, and Tilly began to quote poetry of a morbid tendency. Our parents and guardians entertained different opinions. My uncle Bonsor wanted us to wait till the shares in the Caerlyon-upon-Usk Something or Other Company, in which I was vicariously interested, were at a premium – they have been at a hopeless discount for years. Tilly's papa and mamma called Tilly a girl and self a boy, when we were nothing whatsoever of the kind, and only the most ardent and faithful pair of young lovers that had existed since the time of Abelard and Heloïse, or Florio and Biancafore. As, however, our parents and guardians were not made of adamant or Roman cement, we were not permitted to add another couple to the catalogue of historically unfortunate lovers. Uncle Bonsor and Mr and Mrs Captain Standfast (my Tilly's papa and mamma) at last relented. Much was effected towards their desirable consummation by my arguments against celibacy, contained in eight pages foolscap, and of which I made copies in triplicate for the benefit of our hard-hearted relatives. More was done by Tilly threatening to poison herself. Most, however, was accomplished by our both making up our minds to tell a piece thereof to our parents and guardians, and telling them that if they did not acquiesce in our views we would run away and get married at the very first opportunity. There was no just cause or impediment. We were young, healthy, and had plenty of money between us. Loads of money – as we thought then. As to personal appearance – Tilly was simply lovely, and my whiskers had not been ill spoken of in the best society in Dover. So it was all arranged, and on the twenty-seventh of December 1846, being the morrow of Boxing Day, Alfred Starling, gent., was to be united in the holy bonds of matrimony to Matilda, only daughter of Captain Rockleigh Standfast, R.N., of Snargatestone Villa, Dover.

I had been left an orphan at a very early age, and the guardian of my moderate property (including the shares in the Caerlyon-upon-Usk Something or Other concern), and guardian of my person, was my uncle Bonsor. He sent me to Merchant Taylors', and afterwards for a couple of years to college at Bonn, on the Rhine. He afterwards – to keep me out of mischief, I believe – paid a handsome premium for my entrance into the counting house of Messrs Baum, Brömm and Boompjees, German merchants, of Finsbury Circus, under whose tutelage I did as little as I liked in the corresponding department, and was much envied by my brother salaried clerks. My uncle Bonsor resided chiefly at Dover, where he was making large sums of money by government contracts, whose objects apparently consisted in boring holes in the chalk and then filling them up again. My uncle was perhaps the most respectable man in Europe, and was well known in the city of London as "Respectable Bonsor". He was one of those men who are confidently said to be "good for any amount". He had a waistcoat – worn winter and summer – a waistcoat that wavered in hue between a sunny buff and a stony drab, which looked so ineffably respectable that I am certain if it had been presented at the pay counter of any bank in Lombard Street the clerks would have cashed it at once for any amount of notes or gold demanded. My uncle Bonsor entrenched himself behind this astonishing garment as behind a fortification, and fired guns of respectability at you. That waistcoat had carried resolutions, assuaged the ire of indignant shareholders, given stability to wavering schemes and brought in thumping subscriptions for burnt-out Kaffirs and destitute Fijis. It was a safe waistcoat, and Bonsor was a safe man. He was mixed up with a good many companies, but whenever a projector or promoter came to him with a plan, my responsible uncle would confer with his waistcoat, and within five minutes would either tell the projector or promoter to walk out of his counting house, or put his name down for a thousand pounds. And the scheme was made that Responsible Bonsor put his name down for.

It was arranged that I was to go down to Dover on Christmas Eve, staying at my uncle's, and that we were to dine all together at Captain Standfast's on Christmas Day. Boxing Day was to be devoted to bonnets on the part of my beloved, and to the signing and sealing of certain releases, deeds, covenants and other documents connected with law and money, on the part of self, my uncle and my prospective papa in-law, and on the twenty-seventh we were to be married.

Of course my connection with Messrs Baum, Brömm and Boompjees was brought to an amicable termination. I gave the clerks a grand treat at a hostelry in Newgate Street, and had the pleasure of receiving, at a somewhat late hour, and at least eighty-seven times, a unanimous choral assurance, not unaccompanied by hiccups, that I was a "jolly good fellow". I was unwillingly compelled to defer my departure till the 8.30 p.m. on Christmas Eve, being engaged by a farewell dinner at four, and the mansion of our Mr Max Bompjees, junior and dinner-giving partner in the firm, in Finsbury Circus. A capital dinner it was, and very merry. I left the gentlemen over their wine, and had just time to pop into a cab and catch the mail train at London Bridge.

You know how quickly time passes on a railway journey when one has dined comfortably before starting. I seemed to have been telegraphed down to Dover, so rapidly were the eighty odd miles skimmed over. But it now becomes my duty to impart to you the knowledge of my terrible misfortune. In my youth, a little boy at a preparatory school near Ashford, I had experienced a touch of the dreadful disease of the Kentish marshes. How long this malady had lain concealed in my frame, and by what accident of time or temperature it became again evolved, I had no means of judging, but by the time the train arrived at Dover, I was in the throes of acute ague.

It was a horrible, persistent, regular shivering and shaking, a racking palsy, a violent tremor, accompanied, I am sure, by fever, for my temples throbbed, and I experienced an almost deafening, jarring, rattling noise in the head. My blood seemed all in revolt, and surging backwards and forwards in the distempered current. On the platform I staggered to and fro, and the porter, of whose arm I caught hold to steady myself, seemed, lantern and all, by mere communicated violence, to be shaken and buffeted about as I was. I had always been an abstemious young man, and had not exceeded in the consumption of the hospitable junior partner's rare old hock; besides, for all the noise in my head, I could think and talk – albeit my teeth chattered, and my tongue wagged in my mouth with aguish convulsions. I had never known before that railway porters were a hard-hearted race, but one tall man in velveteen grinned most impertinently as I was helped into a fly, and I am certain that his companion, a short, fat fellow, with a leer in his eye, thrust his tongue into his cheek as he heaped, at my desire, greatcoats and rugs over me, and bade the flyman drive to the Marine Parade, where my uncle resided. I had told everyone at the station about my attack of ague.

"*He's* got his load," I heard the tall porter exclaim, as we drove off. Of course he meant that the flyman had got all my luggage.

It was a dreadful five minutes' ride to my uncle's. The fit was so strong on me that my head and limbs kept bumping against opposite sides of the fly, and once came in contact with the window glass. And the noise in my head never ceased. I stumbled out, somehow, when the vehicle stopped, and, clinging to the knocker of the avuncular door, struck such a quivering peal of blows – I had previously scattered the cabman's fare on the pavement in the attempt to place the money in his hand – that Jakes, my uncle's confidential man, who opened the door, stared with astonishment.

"I'm very ill, Jakes," I stammered, when I had staggered into the hall. "I'm down with the dreadful ague again."

"Yes, sir," answered Jakes, with something like a grin on *his* countenance too. "Compts of the season, sir. Hadn't you better go to bed, sir?"

Now the house was all lit up, for there was to be a snapdragon party, and I knew that my Tilly and all the Standfasts were upstairs with my uncle and his waistcoat, and that they were to wait for my arrival before lighting the bowl. And, ill as I was, I burned to see my darling.

"No, Jakes," I said, "I'll try and bear up. You had better bring me a little cognac, and some very hot water, into the dining room. It will do me good, and the fit may leave me." What would you believe was the reply of this pampered domestic?

"Better not, sir," he had the hardihood to observe. "Christmas time, sir. Plenty more like you. Better go to bed, sir. Think of your head in the morning, sir."

"Fellow…" I began to retort, still violently trembling, when I saw my uncle Bonsor appear at the head of the staircase. There was a group of ladies and gentlemen in the background, and, as well as I could see for shaking, there were the dear golden curls of my Tilly. But her face looked *so* scared and terrified.

"Alfred," said my uncle sternly, from behind his waistcoat, "you ought to be ashamed of yourself. Go to bed directly, sir!"

"Uncle!" I cried, with a desperate attempt to keep myself steady. "Do you think I'm…" Here I made an effort to ascend the staircase, but my foot caught either in the carpet or over one of the confounded brass rods, and, upon my word, I tumbled heels over heels into the hall. And yet, even as I lay recumbent, I shook worse than ever. I heard my uncle's responsible voice ordering the servants to carry me to bed. And I was carried too – Jakes and a long-legged foot page conveying my shaking body to my bedroom.

The night was brief and terrible as in an access of fever, and I lay shaking and chattering in the burning bed. In the morning, my uncle sent word to say that my ague was all nonsense, and that I was to come down to breakfast.

I went down determined on remonstrance, but holding on by the banisters and quivering in every limb. Oh! for the tribulations of that wretched Christmas Day. I was received with sneers, and advised to take very strong tea with a little cognac; yet soon afterwards my uncle shook hands with me, and said that it was only once a year, and that he supposed boys would be boys. Everybody wished me a merry Christmas, but I could only return the compliments of the season in a spasmodic stutter. I took a walk on the pier immediately after breakfast, but I nearly tumbled into the sea, and bumped against so many posts that I had to be led home by a mariner in a yellow sou'wester hat, who insisted that I should give him five shillings to drink my health. Then came a more appalling ordeal. I was to call at Snargatestone Villa to accompany my Tilly and the family to church. To my great relief, though I was shaking in every joint of my fingers and toes, nobody took any notice of my alarming complaint. I began to hope that it might be intermittent, and would pass off, but it wouldn't, and rather increased in violence. My darling girl patted me on the head, and hoped that I was "a good boy now", but when I began shiveringly to explain my attack of ague, she only laughed. We went to church, and then my ague soon brought me into disgrace again. First I created terrible scandal by knocking up against the old pauper women in the free seats, and nearly upsetting the beadle. Then I knocked the church services and hymn books off the ledge of the pew. Then I kicked a hassock from beneath the very knees of my future mamma-in-law. Then I trod – accidentally I declare – on the toes of Mary Seaton, my Tilly's pretty cousin; whereupon she gave a little scream, and my beloved looked daggers at me, and as a climax, in the agony of that extraordinary horizontal shaking fit of mine, I burst the pew door open, and tumbled once more against the beadle, who in stern tones, and in the name of the churchwardens, desired me either to behave myself or to leave the church. I saw that it was no good contending against my complaint, so I did leave, but as I lurched out of the edifice I seemed to see the clergyman shaking in the reading desk, and the clerk wagging to and fro beneath him, while the hatchments and tablets shook on the walls, and the organ in the gallery kept bumping now against the charity boys, now against the charity girls.

It wasn't vertigo: the head swims round under that circumstance. It was clearly ague, and of the very worst description; the body from right to left, and the blood surging in the ears with fever.

At dinner time – my agonies had never ceased, but had not attracted notice – I began literally to put my foot into it again. First, handing Mrs Van Plank of Sandwich down to the dining room – my uncle Bonsor escorted Tilly – I entangled myself in the bugle ornaments which that wealthy but obese woman persisted in wearing, and we came down together with alarming results. I was undermost, shaking miserably, with Mrs Van Plank's large person pressing on my shirt studs. When we were assisted to rise she would not be appeased. She would not join us at dinner. She ordered her fly and returned to Sandwich, and as the carriage drove away, Captain Standfast, R.N., looking at me as savagely as though he would have liked to have me up at the gangway and give me six dozen on the instant, said:

"There goes poor Tilly's diamond bracelet. The old screw won't give it her now. I saw the case on the cushion of the fly."

Was it my fault! Could I help my lamentable ague?

At dinner I went from bad to worse. Item: I spilt two ladlefuls of mock turtle soup over a new damask tablecloth. Item: I upset a glass of Madeira over Mary Seaton's blue moire dress. Item: in a convulsive fit of shaking, I nearly stabbed Lieutenant Lamb, of the Fifty-fourth Regiment, stationed on the Heights, with a silver fork, and finally, in a maniacal attempt to carve a turkey, I sent the entire body of that Christmas bird, with a garland of sausages clinging to it, full butt into the responsible waistcoat of my uncle Bonsor.

The peace was made somehow; I'm sure I don't know in what manner, but half an hour afterwards we were all very pleasant and talkative over our dessert. When I say all, I of course except my happy self. There had been no solution of continuity in my shaking. Somebody, I think, proposed my health. In returning thanks, I hit the proposer a tremendous blow under the left eye with my elbow. Endeavouring to regain my equilibrium, I sent a full glass of claret into the embroidered cambric bosom of that unhappy Lieutenant Lamb. In desperation I caught hold of the tablecloth with both hands. I saw how it would be; the perfidious polished mahogany slid away from my grasp. I turned my foot frantically round the leg of the table nearest me, and with a great crash over went dining table, cut-glass decanters and dessert. Lieutenant Lamb was badly hit across the bridge of the nose with a pair of silver nut crackers, and my uncle Bonsor's head was crowned, in quite a classic manner, with filberts and hot-house grapes.

The bleak December sun rose next morning upon ruin and catastrophe. As well as I can collect my scattered reminiscences of that dismal time, my offences against decorum were once more condoned – not in consequence of my complaint (in which my relatives and friends persisted in disbelieving), but on the ground that it was "only once a year". Lawyers came backwards and forwards to Snargatestone Villa during the forenoon. There was a great production of the boxes, red tape, blue seals, foolscap paper and parchment, and my uncle Bonsor was more responsible than ever. They brought me a paper to sign at last, whispering much among themselves as they did so, and I protest that I could see nothing but a large pool of white, jogging about in a field of green tablecloth, while on the paper an infinity of crabbed characters seemed racing up and down in a crazed and furious manner. I endeavoured to nerve myself to the task of signing, I bit my lips, I clenched my left hand, I tried to screw my wagging head onto my neck, I cramped my toes up in my boots, I held my breath, but was it my fault, when I clutched the pen and tried to write my name, that the abominable goose quill began to dance, and skate, and leap, and plunge, and dig its nibs into the paper, that when, in despair, I seized the inkstand to hold it nearer to the pen, I shook its sable contents, in horrid, horned, tasselled blots, all over a grave legal document? I finished my achievement by inflicting a large splash on my uncle's sacred waistcoat, and hitting Captain Standfast under the third rib with the pen.

"That will do," my papa-in-law cried, collaring me. "Leave the house, scoundrel!"

But I broke from his grasp, and fled to the drawing room, knowing that my Tilly would be there with her bridesmaids and her bonnets.

"Tilly – my adored Matilda!" I cried.

"No further explanation is needed, sir," broke in my beloved, in an inexorable tone. "I have seen and heard quite enough. Alfred Starling, I would sooner wed the meanest hind that gathers samphire on yon cliff than become the bride of a profligate and a drunkard. Go, sir; repent if you can; be ashamed if you can. Henceforth we are strangers. Slave of self-indulgence, adieu for ever!" And she swept out of the room, and I could hear her sobbing her pretty heart out in the boudoir beyond.

I was discarded and expelled for ever from Snargatestone Villa; my uncle Bonsor repudiated me, and disinherited me from any share in his waistcoat; I hurled myself into the next train at the station, and shook all the way back to town. At about dusk on that dreadful Boxing Day, I found myself wandering and jolting about the purlieus of Soho.

From Soho Square – the south-west side, I think – branches a shabby, dingy little court, called Bateman's Buildings. I was standing shivering at the corner of this ill-favoured place, when I stumbled against a gentleman who looked about seven-eighths soldier and one-eighth civilian.

He was a little, dapper, clean-limbed, young-looking old man, with a yellow face, and grey hair and whiskers. Soldiers, save in the cavalry, didn't wear moustaches then. He wore a blue uniform coat, rather white at the seams, and a silver medal with a faded ribbon on his breast. He had a bunch of parti-coloured streamers in his undress cap; he carried a bamboo cane under his arm; on each sleeve he wore golden stripes, much tarnished; on his scarlet collar was embroidered a golden lion; and on his shoulders he had a pair of little, light, golden epaulettes, that very much resembled two sets of teeth from a dentist's glass case, covered with bullion.

"And how are you, my hearty?" said the military gentleman cheerily.

I answered that I was the most miserable wretch in the world; upon which the military gentleman, slapping me on the back and calling me his gallant comrade, asked me to have a pint of beer, warmed with a little spice, and a dash of Old Tom in it, for the sake of Christmas.

"You're a roving buck," observed my new friend. "*I'm* a roving buck. You never happened to have a twin brother named Siph, did you?"

"No," I answered moodily.

"He was as like you as two peas," continued the military gentleman, who had by this time taken my arm, and was leading me all shaking and clattering towards a mouldy little tavern, on whose door jambs were displayed a couple of coloured cartoons, framed and glazed and much fly-blown, and displaying, the one, the presentment of an officer in sky-blue uniform much belaced with silver, and the other a bombardier with an enormous shako ramming the charge into a cannon, the whole surmounted by a place setting forth that smart young men were required for the Honourable East India Company's infantry, cavalry and artillery, and earnestly exhorting all smart young men, as aforesaid, to apply forthwith to Sergeant Major Chutnee, who was always to be heard of at the bar of the Highland Laddie or at the office in Bateman's Buildings.

"The last time I saw him," went on the man with the yellow face and the grey whiskers, when he had tilted me into the Highland Laddie, pinned me, shaking, against the bar counter, and ordered a pint of sophisticated beer, "he had left our service, and was a field marshal in the army of the King of Oude. Many's the time I've seen him with his cocked hat and di'mond epaulettes riding on a white elephant, with five-and-twenty black fellows running after him to brush the flies away and draw the soda-water corks. *Such* brandy he'd have with it, and all through meeting me promiscuous in this very public."

It is useless to prolong the narrative of my conversation with the military gentleman; suffice it to say that within an hour I had taken the fatal shilling, and enlisted in the service of the Honourable East India Company. I was not a beggar. I possessed property, over which my uncle Bonsor had no control. I had not committed any crime, but I felt lost, ruined and desperate, and I enlisted. For a wonder, when I was brought before a magistrate to be attested, and before a surgeon to be examined respecting my sanitary fitness for the service, my ague seemed entirely to have left me. I stood firm and upright in the witness box, and under the measuring standard, and was only deterred by shame and anguish at the misconstruction put upon my conduct at Dover from negotiating for my discharge.

I had scarcely reached the East India recruiting depot at Brentwood, however, before the attacks of ague returned with redoubled severity. At first, on my stating that I had an ear for music, they began to train me for a bandsman, but I could not keep a wind instrument in my hands, and struck those that were played by my comrades from their grasp. Then I was put into the awkward squad among the recruits, and the sergeants caned me, but I could never get beyond the preliminary drill of the goose-step, and I kept my own time, and not the squad's, even then. The depot surgeons wouldn't place the slightest credence in my ague, and the sergeant major of my company reported that I was a skulking, "malingering" impostor. Among my comrades, who despised without pitying me, I got the nickname of "Young-Shivery-Shakery". And the most wonderful thing is that, although I could have procured remittances at any time, the thought of purchasing my discharge never entered my poor, shaking, jarring head.

How they came to send such a trembling infirm creature as a soldier to India, I can't make out, but sent I was, by long sea, in a troop ship, with seven or eight hundred more recruits. My military career in the East came to a very speedy and inglorious termination. We had scarcely arrived at Bombay when the battalion of the European regiment into which I was drafted was sent up-country to the banks of the Sutlej, where the Sikh war was then raging. It was the campaign of Aliwal and Sobraon, but it was very little that I saw of that glorious epoch in our military annals. In contemptuous reference to my nervous disorder, I was only permitted to form part of the baggage guard, and one night, after perhaps ten days' march, throughout which I had shaken most awfully, an attack was made on our rear for mere purposes of plunder by a few rascally badmashes, or thieves. Nothing was easier than to put these paltry scoundrels to the rout. I had been brave enough as a lad and as a young man. I declare that on the present occasion I didn't run away, but my unhappy disease got the mastery of me. I shook my musket out of my hands, my shako off my head, and my knapsack off my back, and my wretched legs shook and jolted me, as it seemed, over miles of arid country. There was some talk of shooting me afterwards, and some of flogging me, but corporal punishment did not exist in the Company's army. They sent me to a vile place of incarceration called a "congee house", where I was fed principally on rice water, and at last I was conveyed to Bombay, tried by court martial, sentenced and publicly drummed out of my regiment as a coward. Yes, I, the son of a gentleman, and the possessor of a genteel private property, had the facings cut off my uniform and, to the sound of the 'Rogues March', was dismissed from the service of the Honourable East India Company with ignominy and disgrace.

I can scarcely tell how I reached England again; whether a berth was given to me, whether I paid for it, or whether I worked my passage home. I can only remember that the ship in which I was a passenger broke her back in Algoa Bay, close to the Cape, and became a total wreck. There was not the slightest danger; we were surrounded by large and small craft and every soul on board was saved, but I shook so terribly and incessantly while the boats were leaving the vessel that the whole ship's company hooted and groaned at me when I was shoved over the side, and I was not allowed to go in the longboat, but was towed alone and aft in the dingy to shore.

I took passage in another ship, which did nothing but shake all the way from the Cape to Plymouth, and at last I reached England. I wrote innumerable letters to my friends and relatives, to Tilly and to my uncle Bonsor, but the only answer I received was a few formal lines from my uncle's lawyer, telling me that my illegible scrawls had come to the hands of the persons for whom they were designed, but that no further notice could be taken of my communications. I was put into the possession of my property to the last penny, but it seems to me that I must have shaken it away either at dice or bagatelle, or ninepins or billiards. And I remember that I never made a stroke at the latter game without hitting my adversary with the cue in the chest, knocking down the marker, sending the balls scudding through the windows, disarranging the scores and cutting holes in the cloth, for which I had to pay innumerable guineas to the proprietor of the rooms.

I remember one day going into a jeweller's shop in Regent Street to purchase a watch key. I had only a silver one now, my gold repeater had been shaken away in some unaccountable manner. It was wintertime, and I wore an overcoat with long loose sleeves. While the shopkeeper was adjusting a key to my watch, my ague fit came upon me with demoniacal ferocity, and, to my horror and dismay, in catching hold of the counter to save myself, I tilted a trayful of diamond rings over. Some fell on the floor, but some – Oh horror and anguish! – fell into the sleeves of my overcoat. I shook so that I seemed to have shaken diamond rings into my hands, my pockets, my very boots. By some uncontrollable impulse I attempted flight, but was seized at the very shop door, and carried, shaking, to the police station.

I was taken before a magistrate, and committed, still shaking, in a van, to jail. I shook for some time in a whitewashed cell, when I was brought up, shaking, to the Central Criminal Court, and placed, shaking, on my trial for an attempted robbery of £1,500 worth of property. The evidence was clear against me. My counsel tried to plead something about "kleptomania", but in vain spoke strongly against my character. I was found guilty, yes, I, the most innocent and unfortunate young man breathing, and sentenced to seven years' transportation! I can recall the awful scene vividly to memory now. The jury in a body were shaking their heads at me. So was the judge, as was my uncle Bonsor, so were the spectators in the gallery, and I was holding on by the spikes on the ledge of the dock, shaking from right to left like ten thousand million aspen leaves. My skull was splitting, my brain was bursting when...

I WOKE.

I was lying in a very uncomfortable position in a first-class carriage of the Dover mail train; everything in the carriage was shaking; the oil was surging to and fro in the lamp; my companions were swaying to and fro, and the sticks and umbrellas were rattling in the network above. The train was "at speed", and my frightful dream was simply due to the violent and unusual oscillation of the train. Then, sitting up, and rubbing my eyes, immensely relieved, but holding on by the compartments near me (so violently did the carriages shake from side to side), I began to remember what I had dreamt or heard of others' dreams before, while at sea or while somebody was knocking loudly at the door, and of the old connections between unusual sound and motion on the thoughts of our innermost souls. And again with odd distinctness I remember that at one period of my distempered vision, namely, when I was attested and examined as a recruit, I had remained perfectly still and steady. This temporary freedom from ague I was fain to ascribe to the customary two or three minutes stoppage of the train at Tunbridge Wells. But, thank Heaven, all this was but a dream!

"Enough to shake one's head off!" exclaimed the testy old lady opposite, alluding to the oscillation of the train, as the guard appeared at the window with a shout of "Do-ver!"

"Well, mum, it had bin a shaking most unusual all the way down," replied that functionary. "Thought we should have bin off the line, more than once. Screws will be looked to tomorrow morning. 'Night, sir!" – this was to me: I knew the man well. "Merry Christmas and a happy new year! You'll be wanting a fly to Snargatestone Villa, won't you, sir? Now, por-ter!"

I did want that fly, and I had it. I paid the driver liberally, and did not scatter his money over the pavement. Mr Jakes insisted upon my having something hot in the dining room the moment I arrived. The weather was so "woundy cold", he said. I joined the merry party upstairs, and was received by my Tilly with open arms, and by my uncle Bonsor with an open waistcoat. I partook in cheerful moderation of the snapdragon festivities of Christmas Eve. We all dined together on Christmas Day, and I helped the soup and carved a turkey beautifully, and on the morrow, Boxing Day, was complimented by my uncle's lawyer on my remarkably neat calligraphy, as displayed in the signatures to the necessary legal documents. On the twenty-seventh of December, 1846,

I was married to my darling Tilly, and was going to live happy ever afterwards, when

I WOKE AGAIN

– really did wake in bed in this Haunted House – and found that I had been very much shaken on the railway coming down, and that there was no marriage, no Tilly, no Mary Seaton, no Van Plank, no anything but myself and the Ghost of the Ague, and the two inner windows of the Double Room rattling like the ghosts of two departed watchmen who wanted spiritual assistance to carry me to the dead and gone old watch house.

4

The Ghost in the Picture Room

by Adelaide Anne Procter

B ELINDA, with a modest self-possession quite her own, promptly answered for this spectre in a low, clear voice:

The lights extinguished: by the hearth I leant,
Half weary with a listless discontent.
The flickering giant shadows, gathering near,
Closed round me with a dim and silent fear;
All dull, all dark; save when the leaping flame,
Glancing, lit up the picture's ancient frame.
Above the hearth it hung. Perhaps the night,
My foolish tremors, or the gleaming light,
Lent power to that portrait dark and quaint –
A portrait such as Rembrandt loved to paint –
The likeness of a nun. I seemed to trace
A world of sorrow in the patient face,
In the thin hands folded across her breast –
Its own and the room's shadow hid the rest.
I gazed and dreamed, and the dull embers stirred,
Till an old legend that I once had heard
Came back to me; linked to the mystic gloom
Of the dark picture in the ghostly room.

In the far south, where clustering views are hung;
Where first the old chivalric lays were sung;
Where earliest smiled that gracious child of France,
Angel and Knight and Fairy, called Romance,
I stood one day. The warm blue June was spread
Upon the earth; blue summer overhead,
Without a child to fleck its radiant flare,
Without a breath to stir its sultry air.

47

All still, all silent, save the sobbing rush
Of rippling waves, that lapsed in silver hush.
Upon the beach; where, glittering towards the strand,
The purple Mediterranean kissed the land.

All still, all peaceful; when a convent chime
Broke on the midday silence for a time,
Then trembling into quiet, seemed to cease,
In deeper silence and more utter peace.
So as I turned to gaze, where, gleaming white,
Half-hid by shadowy trees from passers' sight,
The convent lay, one who had dwelt for long
In that fair home of ancient tale and song,
Who knew the story of each cave and hill,
And every haunting fancy lingering still
Within the land, spake thus to me, and told
The convent's treasured legend, quaint and old:

Long years ago, a dense and flowering wood,
Still more concealed where the white convent stood,
Borne on its perfumed wings the title came:
"Our Lady of the Hawthorns" is its name.
Then did that bell, which still rings out today
Bid all the country rise, or eat, or pray.
Before that convent shrine, the haughty knight
Passed the lone vigil of his perilous fight;
For humbler cottage strife, or village brawl,
The Abbess listened, prayed and settled all.
Young hearts that came, weighed down by love or wrong,
Let her kind presence comforted and strong.
Each passing pilgrim, and each beggar's right
Was food, and rest, and shelter for the night.
But, more than this, the nuns could well impart
The deepest mysteries of the healing art;
Their store of herbs and simples was renowned,
And held in wondering faith for miles around.
Thus strife, love, sorrow, good and evil fate,
Found help and blessing at the convent gate.

Of all the nuns, no heart was half so light,
No eyelids veiling glances half as bright,
No step that glided with such noiseless feet,
No face that looked so tender or so sweet,
No voice that rose in choir so pure, so clear,
No heart to all the others half so dear
(So surely touched by others' pain or woe,
Guessing the grief her young life could not know),
No soul in childlike faith so undefiled,
As Sister Angela's, the "Convent Child".
For thus they loved to call her. She had known
No home, no love, no kindred, save their own –
An orphan, to their tender nursing given,
Child, plaything, pupil, now the bride of heaven.
And she it was who trimmed the lamp's red light
That swung before the altar, day and night.
Her hands it was, whose patient skill could trace
The finest broidery, weave the costliest lace;
But most of all, her first and dearest care,
The office she would never miss or share,
Was every day to weave fresh garlands sweet,
To place before the shrine at Mary's feet.
Nature is bounteous in that region fair,
For even winter has her blossoms there.
Thus Angela loved to count each feast the best,
By telling with what flowers the shrine was dressed.
In pomp supreme the countless roses passed,
Battalion on battalion thronging fast,
Each with a different banner, flaming bright,
Damask, or striped, or crimson, pink or white,
Until they bowed before the new-born Queen,
And the pure virgin lily rose serene.
Though Angela always thought the mother blessed,
Must love the time of her own hawthorns best
Each evening through the year, with equal care,
She placed her flowers; then kneeling down in prayer,
As their faint perfume rose before the shrine,
So rose her thoughts, as pure and as divine.
She knelt until the shades grew dim without,
Till one by one the altar lights shone out,

49

Till one by one the nuns, like shadows dim,
Gathered around to chant their vesper hymn;
Her voice then led the music's winged flight,
And "*Ave, Maris Stella*" filled the night.

But wherefore linger on those days of peace?
When storms draw near, then quiet hours must cease.
War, cruel war, defaced the land, and came
So near the convent with its breath of flame,
That, seeking shelter, frightened peasants fled,
Sobbing out tales of coming fear and dread.
Till after a fierce skirmish, down the road,
One night came straggling soldiers, with their load
Of wounded, dying comrades; and the band,
Half-pleading, yet as if they could command,
Summoned the trembling sisters, craved their care,
Then rode away and left the wounded there.
But soon compassion bade all fear depart,
And bidding every sister do her part,
Some prepare simples, healing salves or bands,
The Abbess chose the more experienced hands
To dress the young wounds needing most skilful care;
Yet even the youngest novice took her share,
And thus to Angela, whose ready will
And pity could not cover lack of skill,
The charge of a young wounded knight must fall,
A case which seemed least dangerous of them all.
Day after day she watched beside his bed,
And first in utter quiet the hours fled:
His feverish moans alone the silence stirred,
Of her soft voice, uttering some pious word.
At last the fever left him; day by day
The hours, no longer silent, passed away.
What could she speak of? First, to still his plaints,
She told him legends of the martyr'd saints;
Described the pangs, which through God's plenteous grace,
Had gained their souls so high and bright a place.
This pious artifice soon found success –
Or so she fancied – for he murmured less.
And so she told the pomp and grand array

50

In which the chapel shone on Easter Day,
Described the vestments, gold, and colours bright,
Counted how many tapers gave their light,
Then in minute detail went on to say,
How the high altar looked on Christmas Day:
The kings and shepherds, all in green and white,
And a large star of jewels gleaming bright.
Then told the sign by which they all had seen,
How even nature loved to greet her Queen,
For, when Our Lady's last procession went
Down the long garden, every head was bent,
And rosary in hand each sister prayed;
As the long floating banners were displayed,
They struck the hawthorn boughs, and showers and showers
Of buds and blossoms strewed her way with flowers.
The knight unwearied listened; till at last,
He too described the glories of his past;
Tourney, and joust, and pageant bright and fair,
And all the lovely ladies who were there.
But half incredulous she heard. Could this –
This be the world? This place of love and bliss!
Where, then, was hid the strange and hideous charm
That never failed to bring the gazer harm?
She crossed herself, yet asked, and listened still,
And still the knight described with all his skill
The glorious world of joy, all joys above,
Transfigured in the golden mist of love.
Spread, spread your wings, ye angel guardians bright,
And shield these dazzling phantoms from her sight!
But no; days passed, matins and vespers rang,
And still the quiet nuns toiled, prayed and sang,
And never guessed the fatal, coiling net
That every day drew near and nearer yet,
Around their darling, for she went and came
About her duties outwardly the same.
The same? Ah, no! Even when she knelt to pray,
Some charméd dream kept all her heart away.
So days went on, until the convent gate
Opened one night. Who durst go forth so late?
Across the moonlit grass, with stealthy tread,

Two silent, shrouded figures passed and fled.
And all was silent, save the moaning seas,
That sobbed and pleaded, and a wailing breeze
That sighed among the perfumed hawthorn trees.

What need to tell that dream so bright and brief,
Of joy unchequered by a dread of grief?
What need to tell how all such dreams must fade,
Before the slow foreboding, dreaded shade,
That floated nearer, until pomp and pride,
Pleasure and wealth, were summoned to her side,
To bid, at least, the noisy hours forget,
And clamour down the whispers of regret.
Still Angela strove to dream, and strove in vain;
Awakened once, she could not sleep again.
She saw, each day and hour, more worthless grown
The heart for which she cast away her own;
And her soul learnt, through bitterest inward strife,
The slight, frail love for which she wrecked her life;
The phantom for which all her hope was given,
The cold bleak earth for which she bartered heaven!
But all in vain; what chance remained? What heart
Would stoop to take so poor an outcast's part?

Years fled, and she grew reckless more and more,
Until the humblest peasant closed his door,
And where she passed, fair dames, in scorn and pride,
Shuddered and drew their rustling robes aside.
At last a yearning seemed to fill her soul,
A longing that was stronger than control:
Once more, just once again, to see the place
That knew her young and innocent; to retrace
The long and weary southern path; to gaze
Upon the haven of her childish days;
Once more beneath the convent roof to lie;
Once more to look upon her home – and die!
Weary and worn – her comrades, chill remorse
And black despair, yet a strange silent force
Within her heart, that drew her more and more –
Onwards she crawled, and begged from door to door.

Weighed down with weary days, her failing strength
Grew less each hour, till one day's dawn at length,
As its first rays flooded the world with light,
Showed the broad waters, glittering blue and bright,
And where, amid the leafy hawthorn wood,
Just as of old the low white convent stood.
Would any know her? Nay, no fear. Her face
Had lost all trace of youth, of joy, of grace,
Of the pure happy soul they used to know –
The novice Angela – so long ago.
She rang the convent bell. The well-known sound
Smote on her heart, and bowed her to the ground.
And she, who had not wept for long dry years,
Felt the strange rush of unaccustomed tears;
Terror and anguish seemed to check her breath,
And stop her heart. Oh God! Could this be death?
Crouching against the iron gate, she laid
Her weary head against the bars, and prayed,
But nearer footsteps drew, then seemed to wait,
And then she heard the opening of the grate,
And saw the withered face, on which awoke
Pity and sorrow, as the portress spoke,
And asked the stranger's bidding: "Take me in,"
She faltered, "Sister Monica, from sin,
And sorrow, and despair, that will not cease;
Oh take me in, and let me die in peace!"
With soothing words the sister bade her wait,
Until she brought the key to unbar the gate.
The beggar tried to thank her as she lay,
And heard the echoing footsteps die away.
But what soft voice was that which sounded near,
And stirred strange trouble in her heart to hear?
She raised her head; she saw – she seemed to know
A face that came from long, long years ago:
Herself; yet not as when she fled away,
The young and blooming novice, fair and gay,
But a grave woman, gentle and serene:
The outcast knew it – *what she might have been*.
But as she gazed and gazed, a radiance bright
Filled all the place with strange and sudden light;

53

The nun was there no longer, but instead,
A figure with a circle round its head,
A ring of glory, and a face so meek,
So soft, so tender… Angela strove to speak,
And stretched her hands out, crying, "Mary, mild,
Mother of mercy, help me! Help your child!"
And Mary answered, "From thy bitter past,
Welcome, my child! Oh, welcome home at last!
I filled thy place. Thy flight is known to none,
For all thy daily duties I have done;
Gathered thy flowers, and prayed, and sang, and slept;
Didst thou not know, poor child, *thy place was kept*?
Kind hearts are here; yet would the tenderest one
Have limits to its mercy: God has none.
And man's forgiveness may be true and sweet,
But yet he stoops to give it. More complete
Is love that lays forgiveness at thy feet,
And pleads with thee to raise it. Only Heaven
Means *crowned*, not *vanquished*, when it says 'Forgiven!'"
Back hurried Sister Monica; but where
Was the poor beggar she left lying there?
Gone, and she searched in vain, and sought the place
For that wan woman, with the piteous face:
But only Angela at the gateway stood,
Laden with hawthorn blossoms from the wood.

And never did a day pass by again,
But the old portress with a sigh of pain
Would sorrow for her loitering, with a prayer
That the poor beggar in her wild despair
Might not have come to any ill, and when
She ended, "God forgive her!" humbly then
Did Angela bow her head, and say "Amen!"
How pitiful her heart was! All could trace
Something that dimmed the brightness of her face
After that day, which none had seen before;
Not trouble – but a shadow – nothing more.

Years passed away. Then, one dark day of dread
Saw all the sisters kneeling round a bed,

Where Angela lay dying: every breath
Struggling beneath the heavy hand of death.
But suddenly a flush lit up her cheek,
She raised her wan right hand and strove to speak.
In sorrowing love they listened; not a sound
Or sigh disturbed the utter silence round;
The very taper's flames were scarcely stirred,
In such hushed awe the sisters knelt and heard.
And thro' that silence Angela told her life:
Her sin, her flight; the sorrow and the strife,
And the return; and then, clear, low and calm,
"Praise God for me, my sisters"; and the psalm
Rang up to heaven, far, and clear, and wide,
Again, and yet again, then sank and died;
While her white face had such a smile of peace,
They saw she never heard the music cease;
And weeping sisters laid her in her tomb,
Crowned with a wreath of perfumed hawthorn bloom.

And thus the legend ended. It may be
Something is hidden in the mystery,
Besides the lesson of God's pardon, shown
Never enough believed, or asked, or known.
Have we not all, amid life's petty strife,
Some pure ideal of a noble life
That once seemed possible? Did we not hear
The flutter of its wings, and feel it near,
And just within our reach? It was. And yet
We lost it in this daily jar and fret,
And now live idle in a vague regret;
But still *our place is kept*, and it will wait,
Ready for us to fill it, soon or late.
No star is ever lost we once have seen,
We always may be what we might have been.
Since good, tho' only thought, his life and breath,
God's life – can always be redeemed from death;
And evil, in its nature, is decay,
And any hour can blot it all away;
The hopes that, lost, in some far distance seem,
May be the truer life, and this the dream.

5

The Ghost in the Cupboard Room

by Wilkie Collins

M R BEAVER, on being "spoke" (as his friend and ally Jack Governor called it), turned out of an imaginary hammock with the greatest promptitude, and went straight on duty. "As it's Nat Beaver's watch," said he, "there shall be no skulking." Jack looked at me, with an expectant and admiring turn of his eye on Mr Beaver, full of complimentary implication. I noticed, by the way, that Jack, in a naval absence of mind with which he is greatly troubled at times, had his arm round my sister's waist. Perhaps this complaint originates in an old nautical requirement of having something to hold on by.

These were the terms of Mr Beaver's revelation to us:

What I have got to put forward will not take very long; and I shall beg leave to begin by going back to last night – just about the time when we all parted from one another to go to bed.

The members of this good company did a very necessary and customary thing last night – they each took a bedroom candlestick, and lit the candle before they went upstairs. I wonder whether any one of them noticed that I left my candlestick untouched, and my candle unlit, and went to bed in a Haunted House, of all the places in the world, in the dark? I don't think any one of them did.

That is, perhaps, rather curious to begin with. It is likewise curious, and just as true, that the bare sight of those candlesticks in the hands of this good company set me in a tremble, and made last night a night's bad dream instead of a night's good sleep. The fact of the matter is – and I give you leave, ladies and gentlemen, to laugh at it as much as you please – that the ghost which haunted *me* last night, which has haunted me off and on for many years past, and which will go on haunting me till I am a ghost myself (and consequently spirit-proof in all respects), is nothing more or less than – a bedroom candlestick.

Yes, a bedroom candlestick and candle, or a flat candlestick and candle – put it which way you like – that is what haunts me. I wish it was something pleasanter and more out of the common way – a beautiful lady, or a mine of gold and silver, or a cellar of wine and a coach and horses, and suchlike. But, being what it is, I must take it for what it is, and make the best of it – and I shall thank you all kindly if you will help me out by doing the same.

I am not a scholar myself, but I make bold to believe that the haunting of any man, with anything under the sun, begins with the frightening of him. At any rate, the haunting of me with a bedroom candlestick and candle began with the frightening of me half out of my life, ladies and gentlemen, and, for the time being, the frightening of me altogether out of my wits. That is not a very pleasant thing to confess to you all, before stating the particulars, but perhaps you will be the readier to believe that I am not a downright coward, because you find me bold enough to make a clean breast of it already, to my own great disadvantage, so far.

These are the particulars, as well as I can put them.

I was apprenticed to the sea when I was about as tall as my own walking stick, and I made good enough use of my time to be fit for a mate's berth at the age of twenty-five years.

It was in the year eighteen hundred and eighteen, or nineteen, I am not quite certain which, that I reached the before-mentioned age of twenty-five. You will please to excuse my memory not being very good for dates, names, numbers, places and suchlike. No fear, though, about the particulars I have undertaken to tell you of; I have got them all shipshape in my recollection; I can see them, at this moment, as clear as noonday in my own mind. But there is a mist over what went before, and, for the matter of that, a mist likewise over much that came after – and it's not very likely to lift at my time of life, is it?

Well, in eighteen hundred and eighteen, or nineteen, when there was peace in our part of the world – and not before it was wanted, you will say – there was fighting of a certain scampering, scrambling kind going on in that old fighting ground, which we seafaring men know by the name of the Spanish Main. The possessions that belonged to the Spaniards in South America had broken into open mutiny and declared for themselves years before. There was plenty of bloodshed between the new government and the old, but the new had got the best of it, for the most part, under one General Bolivar – a famous man in his time, though he seems to have dropped out of people's memories now. Englishmen and Irishmen with a turn for fighting, and nothing particular to do at home, joined the General as volunteers, and some of our merchants here found it a good venture to send supplies across the ocean to the popular side. There was risk enough, of course, in doing this, but where one speculation of the kind succeeded, it made up for two, at the least, that failed. And that's the true principle of trade, wherever I have met with it, all the world over.

Among the Englishmen who were concerned in this Spanish-American business, I, your humble servant, happened in a small way to be one. I was then mate of a brig belonging to a certain firm in the City, which drove a sort of general trade mostly in queer out-of-the-way places, as far from home as possible, and which freighted the brig, in the year I am speaking of, with a cargo of gunpowder for General Bolivar and his volunteers. Nobody knew anything about our instructions, when we sailed, except the captain, and he didn't half seem to like them. I can't rightly say how many barrels of powder we had on board, or how much each barrel held – I only know we had no other cargo. The name of the brig was *The Good Intent* – a queer name enough, you will tell me, for a vessel laden with gunpowder, and sent to help a revolution. And as far as this particular voyage was concerned, so it was. I meant that for a joke, ladies and gentlemen, and I'm sorry to find you don't laugh at it.

The Good Intent was the craziest old tub of a vessel I ever went to sea in, and the worst found in all respects. She was two 230, or 280 tons burden, I forget which, and she had a crew of eight, all told – nothing like as many as we ought by rights to have had to work the brig. However, we were well and honestly paid our wages, and we had to set that against the chance of foundering at sea and, on this occasion, likewise, the chance of being blown up into the bargain. In consideration of the nature of our cargo, we were harassed with new regulations which we didn't at all like, relative to smoking our pipes and lighting our lanterns, and, as usual in such cases, the captain who made the regulations preached what he didn't practise. Not a man of us was allowed to have a bit of lit candle in his hand when he went below – except the skipper, and he used his light, when he turned in, or when he looked over his charts on the cabin table, just as usual. This light was a common kitchen candle, or "dip", of the sort that goes eight or ten to the pound, and it stood in an old battered flat candlestick, with all the japan worn and melted off, and all the tin showing in every respect if he had had a lamp or a lantern, but he stuck to his old candlestick, and that same old candlestick, ladies and gentleman, has ever afterwards stuck to *me*. That's another joke, if you please, and I'm much obliged to Miss Belinda in the corner for being good enough to laugh at it.

Well (I said "well" before, but it's a word that helps a man on like), we sailed in the brig, and shaped our course, first, for the Virgin Islands, in the West Indies, and, after sighting them, we made for the Leeward Islands next, and then stood on due south, till the lookout at the masthead hailed the deck, and said he saw land. That land was the coast of South America. We had had a wonderful voyage so far. We had lost none of our spars or sails, and not a man of us had been harassed to death at the pumps. It wasn't often *The Good Intent* made such a voyage as that, I can tell you.

I was sent aloft to make sure about the land, and I did make sure of it. When I reported the same to the skipper, he went below, and had a look at his letter of instructions and the chart. When he came back on deck again, he altered our course a trifle to the eastwards – I forget the point on the compass, but that don't matter. What I do remember is that it was dark before we closed in with the land. We kept the lead going, and hove the brig to in from four to five fathoms' water, or it might be six – I can't say for certain. I kept a sharp eye to the drift of the vessel, none of us knowing how the currents ran on that coast. We all wondered why the skipper didn't anchor, but he said, no, he must first show a light at the foretop masthead, and wait for an answering light onshore. We did wait, and nothing of the sort appeared. It was starlight and calm. What little wind there was came in puffs off the land. I suppose we waited, drifting a little to the westwards, as I made it out, best part of an hour before anything happened – and then, instead of seeing the light on shore, we saw a boat coming towards us, rowed by two men only.

We hailed them, and they answered, "Friends!" and hailed us by our name. They came on board. One of them was an Irishman, and the other was a coffee-coloured native pilot, who jabbered a little English. The Irishman handed a note to our skipper, who showed it to me. It informed us that the part of the coast we were off then was not safe for discharging our cargo, seeing that spies of the enemy (that is to say, of the old government) had been taken and shot in the neighbourhood the day before. We might trust the brig to the native pilot, and he had his instructions to take us to another part of the coast. The note was signed by the proper parties; so we let the Irishman go back alone in the boat, and allowed the pilot to exercise his lawful authority over the brig. He kept us stretching off from the land till noon the next day – his instructions seemingly ordering our course, in the afternoon, so as to close in with the land again a little before midnight.

This same pilot was about as ill-looking a vagabond as ever I saw – a skinny, cowardly, quarrelsome mongrel, who swore at the men, in the vilest broken English, till they were every one of them ready to pitch him overboard. The skipper kept them quiet, and I kept them quiet, for, the pilot being given us by our instructions, we were bound to make the best of him. Near nightfall, however, with the best will in the world to avoid it, I was unlucky enough to quarrel with him. He wanted to go below with his pipe, and I stopped him, of course, because it was contrary to orders. Upon that, he tried to hustle by me, and I put him away with my hand. I never meant to push him down, but somehow I did. He picked himself up as quick as lightning, and pulled out his knife. I snatched it out of his hand, slapped his murderous face for him and threw his weapon overboard. He gave me one ugly look, and walked aft. I didn't think much of the look then, but I remembered it a little too well afterwards.

We were close in with the land again, just as the wind failed us, between eleven and twelve that night, and dropped our anchor by the pilot's directions. It was pitch dark, and a dead, airless calm. The skipper was on deck with two of our best men for watch. The rest were below, except the pilot, who coiled himself up, more like a snake than a man on the forecastle. It was not my watch till four in the morning. But I didn't like the look of the night, or the pilot, or the state of things generally, and I shook myself down on deck to get my nap there, and be ready for anything at a moment's notice. The last I remember was the skipper whispering to me that he didn't like the look of things either, and that he would go below and consult his instructions again. That is the last I remember, before the slow, heavy, regular roll of the old brig on the groundswell rocked me off to sleep.

I was woke, ladies and gentlemen, by a scuffle on the forecastle, and a gag in my mouth. There was a man on my breast and a man on my legs, and I was bound hand and foot in half a minute. The brig was in the hands of the Spaniards. They were swarming all over her. I heard six heavy splashes in the water, one after another – I saw the captain stabbed to the heart as he came running up the companion – and I heard a seventh splash in the water. Except myself, every soul of us on board had been murdered and thrown into the sea. Why I was left, I couldn't think, till I saw the pilot stoop over me with a lantern, and look to make sure of who I was. There was a devilish grin on his face, and he nodded his head at me, as much as to say, *you* were the man who hustled me down and slapped my face, and I mean to play the game of cat and mouse with *you* in return for it!

I could neither move nor speak, but I could see the Spaniards take off the main hatch and rig the purchases for getting up the cargo. A quarter of an hour afterwards, I heard the sweeps of a schooner, or other small vessel, in the water. The strange craft was laid alongside of us, and the Spaniards set to work to discharge our cargo into her. They all worked hard except the pilot, and he came, from time to time, with his lantern, to have another look at me, and to grin and nod always in the same devilish way. I am old enough now not to be ashamed of confessing the truth, and I don't mind acknowledging that the pilot frightened me.

The fright, and the bonds, and the gag, and the not being able to stir hand or foot, had pretty nigh worn me out, by the time the Spaniards gave over work. This was just as the dawn broke. They had shifted a good part of our cargo on board their vessel, but nothing like all of it, and they were sharp enough to be off with what they had got before daylight. I need hardly say that I had made up my mind, by this time, to the worst I could think of. The pilot, it was clear enough, was one of the spies of the enemy, who had wormed himself into the confidence of our consignees without being suspected. He, or more likely his employers, had got knowledge enough of us to suspect what our cargo was; we had been anchored for the night in the safest berth for them to surprise us in, and we had paid the penalty of having a small crew, and consequently an insufficient watch. All this was clear enough – but what did the pilot mean to do with *me*?

On the word of a man, it makes my flesh creep now only to tell you what he did with me.

After all the rest of them were out of the brig, except the pilot and two Spanish seamen, these last took me up, bound and gagged as I was, lowered me into the hold of the vessel, and laid me along on the floor, lashing me to it with ropes' ends, so that I could not roll myself fairly over, so as to change my place. Then they left me. Both of them were the worse for liquor, but the devil of a pilot was sober – mind that! – as sober as I am at the present moment.

I lay in the dark for a little while, with my heart thumping as if it was going to jump out of me. I lay about five minutes so, when the pilot came down into the hold alone. He had the captain's cursed flat candlestick and a carpenter's awl in one hand, and a long thin twist of cotton yarn, well oiled, in the other. He put the candlestick, with a new "dip" lit in it, down on the floor, about two feet from my face, and close against the side of the vessel. The light was feeble enough, but it was sufficient to show a dozen barrels of gunpowder or more, left all around me in the hold of the brig. I began to suspect what he was after, the moment I noticed the barrels. The horrors laid hold of me from head to foot, and the sweat poured off my face like water.

I saw him go next to one of the barrels of powder standing against the side of the vessel, in a line with the candle, and about three feet, or rather better, away from it. He bored a hole in the side of the barrel with his awl, and the horrid powder came trickling out, as black as hell, and dripped into the hollow of his hand, which he held to catch it. When he had got a good handful, he stopped up the hole by jamming one end of his oiled twist of cotton yarn fast into it, and he then rubbed the powder into the whole length of the yarn, till he had blackened every hair's breadth of it. The next thing he did – as true as I sit here, as true as the heaven above us all – the next thing he did was to carry the free end of his long, lean, black, frightful slow-match to the lit candle alongside my face, and to tie it, in several folds, round the tallow dip, about a third of the distance down, measuring from the flame of the wick to the lip of the candlestick. He did that; he looked to see that my lashings were all safe, and then he put his face down close to mine, and whispered in my ear, "Blow up with the brig!"

He was on deck again the moment after, and he and the two others shoved the hatch on over me. At the furthest end from where I lay, they had not fitted it down quite true, and I saw a blink of daylight glimmering in when I looked in that direction. I heard the sweeps of the schooner fall into the water – splash! splash! – fainter and fainter, as they swept the vessel out in the dead calm, to be ready for the wind in the offing. Fainter and fainter – splash! splash! – for a quarter of an hour or more.

While these sounds were in my ears, my eyes were fixed on the candle. It had been freshly lit – if left to itself it would burn for between six and seven hours – the slow-match was twisted round it about a third of the way down – and therefore the flame would be about two hours reaching it. There I lay, gagged, bound, lashed to the floor, seeing my own life burning down with the candle by my side – there I lay, alone on the sea, doomed to be blown to atoms, and to see that doom drawing on, nearer and nearer with every fresh second of time, through nigh on two hours to come, powerless to help myself and speechless to call for help to others. The wonder to me is that I didn't cheat the flame, the slow-match and the powder, and die of the horror of my situation before my first half-hour was out in the hold of the brig.

I can't exactly say how long I kept the command of my senses after I had ceased to hear the splash of the schooner's sweeps in the water.

63

I can trace back everything I did and everything I thought up to a certain point, but once past that, I get all abroad, and lose myself in my memory now, much as I lost myself in my own feelings at the time.

The moment the hatch was covered over me, I began, as every other man would have begun in my place, with a frantic effort to free my hands. In the mad panic I was in, I cut my flesh with the lashings as if they had been knife blades, but I never stirred them. There was less chance still of freeing my legs, or of tearing myself from the fastenings that held me to the floor. I gave in when I was all but suffocated for want of breath. The gag, you will please to remember, was a terrible enemy to me; I could only breathe freely through my nose – and that is but a poor vent when a man is straining his strength as far as ever it will go.

I gave in, and lay quiet, and got my breath again, my eyes glaring and straining at the candle all the time. While I was staring at it, the notion struck me of trying to blow out the flame by pumping a long breath at it suddenly through my nostrils. It was too high above me, and too far away from me, to be reached in that fashion. I tried, and tried, and tried – and then I gave in again and lay quiet again, always with my eyes glaring at the candle and the candle glaring at *me*. The splash of the schooner's sweeps was very faint by this time. I could only just hear them in the morning stillness. Splash! splash! – fainter and fainter – splash! splash!

Without exactly feeling my mind going, I began to feel it getting queer, as early as this. The snuff of the candle was growing taller and taller, and the length of tallow between the flame and the slow-match, which was the length of my life, was getting shorter and shorter. I calculated that I had rather less than an hour and a half to live. An hour and a half! Was there a chance, in that time, of a boat pulling off to the brig from shore? Whether the land near which the vessel was anchored was in possession of our side, or in possession of the enemy's side, I made it out that they must, sooner or later, send to hail the brig, merely because she was a stranger in those parts. The question for *me* was how soon? The sun had not risen yet, as I could tell by looking through the chink in the hatch. There was no coast village near us, as we all knew, before the brig was seized, by seeing no lights on shore. There was no wind, as I could tell by listening, to bring any strange vessel near. If I had had six hours to live, there might have been a chance for me, reckoning from sunrise to noon. But with an hour and a half, which had dwindled to an hour and a quarter by this time – or, in other words, with the earliness of the morning, the uninhabited coast and the dead calm all against me – there was not the ghost of a chance. As I felt that, I had another struggle – the last – with my bonds, and only cut myself the deeper for my pains.

I gave in once more, and lay quiet, and listened for the splash of the sweeps. Gone! Not a sound could I hear but the blowing of a fish, now and then, on the surface of the sea, and the creak of the brig's crazy old spars, as she rolled gently from side to side with the little swell there was on the quiet water.

An hour and a quarter. The wick grew terribly, as the quarter slipped away, and the charred top of it began to thicken and spread out mushroom-shape. It would fall off soon. Would it fall off red-hot, and would the swing of the brig cant it over the side of the candle and let it down on the slow-match? If it would, I had about ten minutes to live instead of an hour. This discovery set my mind for a minute on a new tack altogether. I began to ponder with myself what sort of a death blowing up might be. Painful? Well, it would be, surely, too sudden for that. Perhaps just one crash, inside me, or outside me, or both, and nothing more? Perhaps not even a crash; that and death and the scattering of this living body of mine into millions of fiery sparks might all happen the same instant? I couldn't make it out; I couldn't settle how it would be. The minute of calmness in my mind left it, before I had half done thinking, and I got all abroad again.

When I came back to my thoughts, or when they came back to me (I can't say which), the wick was awfully tall, the flame was burning with a smoke above it, the charred top was broad and red, and heavily spreading out to its fall. My despair and horror at seeing it took me in a new way, which was good and right, at any rate, for my poor soul. I tried to pray – in my own heart, you will understand, for the gag put all lip-praying out of my power. I tried, but the candle seemed to burn it up in me. I struggled hard to force my eyes from the slow, murdering flame, and to look up through the chink in the hatch at the blessed daylight. I tried once, tried twice, and gave it up. I tried next only to shut my eyes, and keep them shut – once – twice – and the second time I did it. "God bless our mother, and sister Lizzie; God keep them both, and forgive *me*." This was all I had time to say, in my own heart, before my eyes opened again, in spite of me, and the flame of the candle flew into them, flew all over me and burned up the rest of my thoughts in an instant.

I couldn't hear the fish blowing now; I couldn't hear the creak of the spars; I couldn't think; I couldn't feel the sweat of my own death agony on my face – I could only look at the heavy, charred top of the wick. It swelled, tottered, bent over to one side, dropped – red-hot at the moment of its fall – black and harmless, even before the swing of the brig had canted it over into the bottom of the candlestick.

I caught myself laughing. Yes! Laughing at the safe fall of the bit of wick. But for the gag I should have screamed with laughing. As it was, I shook with it inside me – shook till the blood was in my head, and I was all but suffocated for want of breath. I had just sense enough left to feel that my own horrid laughter, at that awful moment, was a sign of my brain going at last. I had just sense enough left to make another struggle before my mind broke loose like a frightened horse, and ran away with me.

One comforting look at the blink of daylight through the hatch was what I tried for once more. The fight to force my eyes from the candle and to get that one look at the daylight was the hardest I had had yet, and I lost the fight. The flame had hold of my eyes as fast as the lashings had hold of my hands. I couldn't look away from it. I couldn't even shut my eyes, when I tried that next, for the second time. There was the wick, growing tall once more. There was the space shortened to an inch or less. How much life did that inch leave me? Three-quarters of an hour? Half an hour? Fifty minutes? Twenty minutes? Steady! An inch of tallow candle would burn no longer than twenty minutes. An inch of tallow! Wonderful! Why, the greatest king that sits on a throne can't keep a man's body and soul together, and here's an inch of tallow that can do what the king can't! There's something to tell Mother, when I get home, which will surprise her more than all the rest of my voyages put together. I laughed inwardly again at the thought of that, and shook and swelled and suffocated myself, till the light of the candle leapt in through my eyes, and licked up the laughter, and burned it out of me, and made me all empty, and cold, and quiet once more.

Mother and Lizzie. I don't know when they came back, but they did come back – not, as it seemed to me, into my mind this time, but right down bodily before me, in the hold of the brig.

Yes – sure enough, there was Lizzie, just as light-hearted as usual, laughing at me. Laughing! Well why not? Who is to blame Lizzie for thinking I'm lying on my back, drunk in the cellar, with the beer barrels all round me? Steady! She's crying now – spinning round and round in a fiery mist, wringing her hands, screeching out for help – fainter and fainter, like the splash of the schooner's sweeps. Gone! Burnt up in the fiery mist. Mist? fire? No: neither one nor the other. It's Mother makes the light – Mother knitting, with ten flaming points at the ends of her fingers and thumbs, and slow-matches hanging in bunches all round her face instead of her own grey hair. Mother in her old armchair, and the pilot's long skinny hands hanging over the back of the chair, dripping with gunpowder. No! No gunpowder, no chair, no Mother – nothing but the pilot's face, shining *red-hot*, like a sun, in the fiery mist, turning upside down in the fiery mist, running backwards and forwards along the slow-match, in the fiery mist, spinning millions of miles in a minute, in the fiery mist – spinning itself smaller and smaller into one tiny point, and that point darting on a sudden straight into my head – and then, all fire and all mist – no hearing, no seeing, no thinking, no feeling – the brig, the sea, my own self, the whole world, all gone together!

After what I've just told you, I know nothing and remember nothing, till I woke up, as it seemed to me in a comfortable bed, with two rough and ready men like myself sitting on each side of my pillow, and a gentleman standing watching me at the foot of the bed. It was about seven in the morning. My sleep (or what seemed like my sleep to me) had lasted better than eight months – I was among my own countrymen in the island of Trinidad – the men at each side of my pillow were my keepers, turn and turn about – and the gentleman standing at the foot of the bed was the doctor. What I said and did in those eight months, I never have known and never shall. I woke out of it as if it had been one long sleep – that's all I know.

It was another two months or more before the doctor thought it safe to answer the questions I asked him.

The brig had been anchored, just as I had supposed, off a part of the coast which was lonely enough to make the Spaniards pretty sure of no interruption, so long as they managed their murderous work quietly under cover of night. My life had not been saved from the shore, but from the sea. An American vessel, becalmed in the offing, had made out the brig as the sun rose, and the captain, having his time on his hands in consequence of the calm, and seeing the vessel anchored where no vessel had any reason to be, had manned one of his boats and sent his mate with it, to look a little closer into the matter, and bring back a report of what he saw. What he saw, when he and his men found the brig deserted and boarded her, was a gleam of candlelight through the chink in the hatchway. The flame was within about a thread's breadth of the slow-match, when he lowered himself into the hold, and if he had not had the sense and coolness to cut the match in two with his knife, before he touched the candle, he and his men might have been blown up along with the brig, as well as me. The match caught and turned into sputtering red fire, in the very act of putting the candle out, and if the communication with the powder barrel had not been cut off, the Lord only knows what might have happened.

What became of the Spanish schooner and the pilot I have never heard from that day to this. As for the brig, the Yankees took her, as they took me, to Trinidad, and claimed their salvage, and got it, I hope, for their own sakes. I was landed just in the same state as when they rescued me from the brig, that is to say, clean out of my senses. But please to remember it was a long time ago, and, take my word for it, I was discharged cured, as I have told you. Bless your hearts, I'm all right now, as you may see. I'm a little shaken by telling the story, ladies and gentlemen – a little shaken, that's all.

6

The Ghost in Master B.'s Room

by Charles Dickens

I T BEING NOW MY OWN TURN, I "took the word", as the French say, and
went on:

When I established myself in the triangular garret which had gained so
distinguished a reputation, my thoughts naturally turned to Master B. My
speculations about him were uneasy and manifold. Whether his Christian
name was Benjamin, Bissextile (from his having been born in Leap Year),
Bartholomew or Bill. Whether the initial letter belonged to his family
name, and that was Baxter, Black, Brown, Barker, Buggins, Baker or Bird.
Whether he was a foundling, and had been baptized B. Whether he was a
lion-hearted boy, and B. was short for Briton, or for Bull. Whether he could
possibly have been kith and kin to an illustrious lady who brightened my
own childhood, and had come to the blood of the brilliant Mother Bunch?

With these profitless meditations I tormented myself much. I also carried
the mysterious letter into the appearance and pursuits of the deceased,
wondering whether he dressed in Blue, wore Boots (he couldn't have
been Bald), was a boy of Brains, liked Books, was good at Bowling, had
any skill as a Boxer, ever in his Buoyant Boyhood Bathed from a Bathing
machine at Bognor, Bangor, Bournemouth, Brighton or Broadstairs, like
a Bounding Billiard Ball?

So, from the first, I was haunted by the letter B.

It was not long before I remarked that I never by any hazard had a
dream of Master B., or of anything belonging to him. But the instant I
awoke from sleep, at whatever hour of the night, my thoughts took him
up, and roamed away, trying to attach his initial letter to something that
would fit it and keep it quiet.

For six nights, I had been worried thus in Master B.'s room, when I
began to perceive that things were going wrong.

The first appearance that presented itself was early in the morning,
when it was but just daylight and no more. I was standing shaving at my

glass, when I suddenly discovered, to my consternation and amazement, that I was shaving – not myself – I am fifty – but a boy. Apparently Master B.?

I trembled and looked over my shoulder – nothing there. I looked again in the glass, and distinctly saw the features and expression of a boy, who was shaving, not to get rid of a beard, but to get one. Extremely troubled in my mind, I took a few turns in the room, and went back to the looking glass, resolved to steady my hand and complete the operation in which I had been disturbed. Opening my eyes, which I had shut while recovering my firmness, I now met in the glass, looking straight at me, the eyes of a young man of four- or five-and-twenty. Terrified by this new ghost, I closed my eyes, and made a strong effort to recover myself. Opening them again, I saw, shaving his cheek in the glass, my father, who has long been dead. Nay, I even saw my grandfather too, whom I never did see in my life.

Although naturally much affected by these remarkable visitations, I determined to keep my secret, until the time agreed upon for the present general disclosure. Agitated by a multitude of curious thoughts, I retired to my room, that night, prepared to encounter some new experience of a spectral character. Nor was my preparation needless, for, waking from an uneasy sleep at exactly two o'clock in the morning, what were my feelings to find that I was sharing my bed with the skeleton of Master B.!

I sprang up, and the skeleton sprang up also. I then heard a plaintive voice saying, "Where am I? What is become of me?" and, looking hard in that direction, perceived the ghost of Master B.

The young spectre was dressed in an obsolete fashion – or rather, was not so much dressed as put into a case of inferior pepper-and-salt cloth, made horrible by means of shining buttons. I observed that these buttons went, in a double row, over each shoulder of the young ghost, and appeared to descend his back. He wore a frill round his neck. His right hand (which I distinctly noticed to be inky) was laid upon his stomach; connecting this action with some feeble pimples on his countenance, and his general air of nausea, I concluded this ghost to be the ghost of a boy who had habitually taken a great deal too much medicine.

"Where am I?" said the little spectre, in a pathetic voice. "And why was I born in the calomel days, and why did I have all that calomel given me?"

I replied, with sincere earnestness, that upon my soul I couldn't tell him.

"Where is my little sister," said the ghost, "and where my angelic little wife, and where is the boy I went to school with?"

I entreated the phantom to be comforted, and above all things to take heart respecting the loss of the boy he went to school with. I represented to him that probably that boy never did, within human experience, come out well, when discovered. I urged that I myself had, in later life, turned up several boys whom I went to school with, and none of them had at all answered. I expressed my humble belief that that boy never did answer. I represented that he was a mythic character, a delusion and a snare. I recounted how, the last time I found him, I found him at a dinner party behind a wall of white cravat, with an inconclusive opinion on every possible subject, and a power of silent boredom absolutely titanic. I related how, on the strength of our having been together at "Old Doylance's", he had asked himself to breakfast with me (a social offence of the largest magnitude); how, fanning my weak embers of belief in Doylance's boys, I had let him in; and how he had proved to be a fearful wanderer about the earth, pursuing the race of Adam with inexplicable notions concerning the currency, and with a proposition that the Bank of England should, on pain of being abolished, instantly strike off and circulate God knows how many thousand millions of ten and sixpenny notes.

The ghost heard me in silence, and with a fixed stare. "Barber!" it apostrophized me when I had finished.

"Barber?" I repeated – for I am not of that profession.

"Condemned," said the ghost, "to shave a constant change of customers – now me – now a young man – now thyself as thou art – now thy father – now thy grandfather; condemned, too, to lie down with a skeleton every night, and to rise with it every morning…"

(I shuddered on hearing this dismal announcement).

"Barber! Pursue me!"

I had felt, even before the words were uttered, that I was under a spell to pursue the phantom. I immediately did so, and was in Master B.'s room no longer.

Most people know what long and fatiguing night journeys had been forced upon the witches who used to confess, and who, no doubt, told the exact truth – particularly as they were always assisted with leading questions, and the Torture was always ready. I asseverate that, during my occupation of Master B.'s room, I was taken by the ghost that haunted it on expeditions fully as long and wild as any of those. Assuredly, I was presented to no shabby old man with a goat's horns and tail (something

71

between Pan and an old clothes-man), holding conventional receptions, as stupid as those of real life and less decent, but I came upon other things which appeared to me to have more meaning.

Confident that I speak the truth and shall be believed, I declare without hesitation that I followed the ghost, in the first instance on a broomstick, and afterwards on a rocking horse. The very smell of the animal's paint – especially when I brought it out, by making him warm – I am ready to swear to. I followed the ghost afterwards in a hackney coach – an institution with the peculiar smell of which the present generation is unacquainted, but to which I am again ready to swear as a combination of stable, dog with the mange and very old bellows. (In this, I appeal to previous generations to confirm or refute me.) I pursued the phantom on a headless donkey: at least, upon a donkey who was so interested in the state of his stomach that his head was always down there, investigating it; on ponies expressly born to kick up behind; on roundabouts and swings from fairs; in the first cab – another forgotten institution where the fare regularly got into bed, and was tucked up with the driver.

Not to trouble you with a detailed account of all my travels in pursuit of the ghost of Master B., which were longer and more wonderful than those of Sinbad the Sailor, I will confine myself to one experience from which you may judge of many.

I was marvellously changed. I was myself, yet not myself. I was conscious of something within me, which has been the same all through my life, and which I have always recognized under all its phases and varieties as never altering, and yet I was not the I who had gone to bed in Master B.'s room. I had the smoothest of faces and the shortest of legs, and I had taken another creature like myself, also with the smoothest of faces and the shortest of legs, behind a door, and was confiding to him a proposition of the most astounding nature.

This proposition was that we should have a seraglio.

The other creature assented warmly. He had no notion of respectability, neither had I. It was the custom of the East, it was the way of the good Caliph Haroun Alraschid (let me have the corrupted name again for once, it is so scented with sweet memories!), the usage was highly laudable, and most worthy of imitation. "Oh yes! Let us," said the other creature with a jump, "have a seraglio."

It was not because we entertained the faintest doubts of the meritorious character of the Oriental establishment we proposed to import that we perceived it must be kept a secret from Miss Griffin. It was because we knew Miss Griffin to be bereft of human sympathies, and incapable of appreciating the greatness of the great Haroun. Mystery impenetrably shrouded from Miss Griffin then, let us entrust it to Miss Bule.

We were ten in Miss Griffin's establishment by Hampstead Ponds – eight ladies and two gentlemen. Miss Bule, whom I judge to have attained a ripe age of eight or nine, took the lead in society. I opened the subject to her in the course of the day, and proposed that she should become the Favourite.

Miss Bule, after struggling with the diffidence so natural to, and charming in, her adorable sex, expressed herself as flattered by the idea, but wished to know how it was proposed to provide for Miss Pipson? Miss Bule – who was understood to have vowed towards that young lady a friendship, halves and no secrets, until death, on the *Church Service and Lessons* complete in two volumes with case and lock – Miss Bule said she could not, as the friend of Pipson, disguise from herself, or me, that Pipson was not one of the common.

Now, Miss Pipson, having curly light hair and blue eyes (which was my idea of anything mortal and feminine that was called Fair), I promptly replied that I regarded Miss Pipson in the light of the Fair Circassian.

"And what then?" Miss Bule pensively asked.

I replied that she must be inveigled by a merchant, brought to me veiled and purchased as a slave.

(The other creature had already fallen into the second male place in the state, and was set apart from Grand Vizier. He afterwards resisted this disposal of events, but had his hair pulled until he yielded.)

"Shall I be not jealous?" Miss Bule enquired, casting down her eyes.

"Zobeide, no," I replied, "you will ever be the favourite Sultana; the first place in my heart, and on my throne, will be ever yours."

Miss Bule, upon that assurance, consented to propound the idea to her seven beautiful companions. It occurring to me, in the course of the same day, that we knew we could trust a grinning and good-natured soul called Tabby, who was the serving drudge of the house, and had no more figure than one of the beds, and upon whose face there was always more or less blacklead, I slipped into Miss Bule's hand after supper a little note to that effect, dwelling on the blacklead as being in a manner deposited by the finger of Providence, pointing out for Mesrour, the celebrated chief of the Blacks of the Harem.

There were difficulties in the formation of the desired institution, as there are in all combinations. The other creature showed himself of a low character and, when defeated in aspiring to the throne, pretended to have conscientious scruples about prostrating himself before the Caliph, wouldn't call him Commander of the Faithful, spoke of him slightingly and inconsistently as a mere "chap", said he, the other creature, "wouldn't play" – play! – and was otherwise coarse and offensive. This meanness of disposition was, however, put down by the general indignation of a united seraglio, and I became blessed in the smiles of eight of the fairest of the daughters of men.

The smiles could only be bestowed when Miss Griffin was looking another way, and only then in a very wary manner, for there was a legend among the followers of the Prophet that she saw with a little round ornament in the middle of the pattern on the back of her shawl. But every day after dinner, for an hour, we were all together, and then the Favourite and the rest of the Royal Harem competed who should most beguile the leisure of the Serene Haroun reposing from the cares of state – which were generally, as in most affairs of state, of an arithmetical character, the Commander of the Faithful being a fearful boggler at a sum.

On these occasions, the devoted Mesrour, chief of the Blacks of the Harem, was always in attendance (Miss Griffin usually ringing for that officer, at the same time, with great vehemence), but never acquitted himself in a manner worthy of his historical reputation. In the first place, his bringing a broom into the divan of the Caliph, even when Haroun wore on his shoulders the red robe of anger (Miss Pipson's pelisse), though it might be got over for the moment, was never to be quite satisfactorily accounted for. In the second place, his breaking out into grinning exclamations of "Lork you pretties!" was neither Eastern nor respectful. In the third place, when specially instructed to say "Bismillah!" he always said "Hallelujah!" This officer, unlike his class, was too good-humoured altogether, kept his mouth open far too wide, expressed approbation to an incongruous extent, and even once – it was on the occasion of the purchase of the Fair Circassian for five hundred thousand purses of gold, and cheap, too – embraced the slave, the Favourite, and the Caliph, all round. (Parenthetically let me say God bless Mesrour, and may there have been sons and daughters on that tender bosom, softening many a hard day since!)

Miss Griffin was a model of propriety, and I am at a loss to imagine what the feelings of the virtuous woman would have been if she had known, when she paraded us down the Hampstead road two and two, that she was walking with a stately step at the head of Polygamy and Mahommedanism. I believe that a mysterious and terrible joy with which the contemplation of Miss Griffin, in this unconscious state, inspired us, and a grim sense prevalent among us that there was a dreadful power in our knowledge of what Miss Griffin (who knew all things that could be learnt out of a book) didn't know, were the mainspring of the preservation of our secret. It was wonderfully kept, but was once upon the verge of self-betrayal. The danger and escape occurred upon a Sunday. We were all ten ranged in a conspicuous part of the gallery at church, with Miss Griffin at our head – as we were every Sunday – advertising the establishment in an unsecular sort of way – when the description of Solomon in his domestic glory happened to be read. The moment that monarch was thus referred to, conscience whispered me, "Thou, too, Haroun!" The officiating minister had a cast in his eye, and it assisted conscience by giving him the appearance of reading personally at me. A crimson blush, attended by a fearful perspiration, suffused my features. The Grand Vizier became more dead than alive, and the whole seraglio reddened as if the sunset of Baghdad shone direct upon their lovely faces. At this portentous time the awful Griffin rose, and balefully surveyed the children of Islam. My own impression was that Church and State had entered into a conspiracy with Miss Griffin to expose us, and that we should all be put into white sheets, and exhibited in the centre aisle. But so Westerly – if I may be allowed the expression as opposite to Eastern associations – was Miss Griffin's sense of rectitude, that she merely suspected apples, and we were saved.

I have called the seraglio united. Upon the question, solely, whether the Commander of the Faithful durst exercise a right of kissing in that sanctuary of the palace, were its peerless intimates divided. Zobeide asserted a counter-right in the Favourite to scratch, and the Fair Circassian put her face, for refuge, into a green baize bag, originally designed for books. On the other hand, a young antelope of transcendent beauty from the fruitful plains of Camden Town (whence she had been brought, by traders, in the half-yearly caravan that crossed the intermediate desert after the holidays), held more liberal opinions, but stipulated for limiting the benefit of them to that dog, and son of a dog, the Grand Vizier – who had no rights, and was not in question. At length, the difficulty was compromised by the installation of a very youthful slave as deputy. She, raised upon a stool, officially received upon her cheeks the salutes intended by the gracious Haroun for other Sultanas, and was privately rewarded from the coffers of the Ladies of the Harem.

And now it was, at the full height of enjoyment of my bliss, that I became heavily troubled. I began to think of my mother, and what she would say to my taking home at midsummer eight of the most beautiful daughters of men, but all unexpected. I thought of the number of beds we made up at our house, of my father's income and of the baker, and my despondency redoubled. The seraglio and malicious Vizier, divining the cause of their Lord's unhappiness, did their utmost to augment it. They professed unbounded felicity, and declared that they would live and die with him. Reduced to the utmost wretchedness by these protestations of attachment, I lay awake, for hours at a time, ruminating on my frightful lot. In my despair, I think I might have taken an early opportunity of falling on my knees before Miss Griffin, avowing my resemblance to Solomon, and praying to be dealt with according to the outraged laws of my country, if an unthought-of means of escape had not opened before me.

One day, we were out walking, two and two – on which occasion the Vizier had his usual instructions to take note of the boy at the turnpike, and if he profanely gazed (which he always did) at the beauties of the harem, to have him bowstrung in the course of the night – and it happened that our hearts were veiled in gloom. An unaccountable action on the part of the antelope had plunged the state into disgrace. That charmer, on the representation that the previous day was her birthday, and that vast treasures had been sent in a hamper for its celebration (both baseless assertions), had secretly but most pressingly invited thirty-five neighbouring princes and princesses to a ball and supper, with a special stipulation that they were "not to be fetched till twelve". This wandering of the antelope's fancy led to the surprising arrival at Miss Griffin's door, in divers equipages and under various escorts, of a great company in full dress, who were deposited on the top step in a flush of high expectancy, and who were dismissed in tears. At the beginning of the double knocks attendant on these ceremonies, the antelope had retired to a back attic, and bolted herself in, and at every new arrival, Miss Griffin had gone so much more and more distracted, that at last she had been seen to tear her front. Ultimate capitulation on the part of the offender had been followed by solitude in the linen closet, bread and water, and a lecture to all of vindictive length, in which Miss Griffin had used the expressions: firstly, "I believe you all of you knew of it", secondly, "Every one of you is as wicked as another", thirdly, "A pack of little wretches".

Under these circumstances, we were walking drearily along, and I especially, with my Mussulman responsibilities heavy on me, was in a very low state of mind, when a strange man accosted Miss Griffin, and, after walking on at her side for a little while and talking with her, looked at me. Supposing him to be a minion of the law, and that my hour was come, I instantly ran away, with a general purpose of making for Egypt.

The whole seraglio cried out, when they saw me making off as fast as my legs would carry me (I had an impression that the first turning on the left, and round by the public house, would be the shortest way to the Pyramids), Miss Griffin screamed after me, the faithless Vizier ran after me and the boy at the turnpike dodged me into a corner, like a sheep, and cut me off. Nobody scolded me when I was taken and brought back; Miss Griffin only said, with a stunning gentleness, This was very curious! Why had I run away when the gentleman looked at me?

If I had had any breath to answer with, I dare say I should have made no answer; having no breath, I certainly made none. Miss Griffin and the strange man took me between them, and walked me back to the palace in a sort of state, but not at all (as I couldn't help feeling, with astonishment), in culprit state.

When we got there, we went into a room by ourselves, and Miss Griffin called in to her assistance Mesrour, chief of the dusky guards of the harem. Mesrour, on being whispered to, began to shed tears.

"Bless you, my precious!" said that officer, turning to me, "your Pa's took bitter bad!"

I asked, with a fluttered heart, "Is he very ill?"

"Lord temper the wind to you, my lamb!" said the good Mesrour, kneeling down, that I might have a comforting shoulder for my head to rest on. "Your Pa's dead!"

Haroun Alraschid took to flight at the words; the seraglio vanished; from that moment, I never again saw one of the eight of the fairest of the daughters of men.

I was taken home, and there was Debt at home as well as Death, and we had a sale there. My own little bed was as superciliously looked upon by a Power unknown to me, hazily called "The Trade", that a brass coal scuttle, a roasting jack and a birdcage were obliged to be put into it to make a lot of it, and then it went for a song. So I heard mentioned, and I wondered what song, and thought what a dismal song it must have been to sing!

Then I was sent to a great, cold, bare school of big boys; where everything to eat and wear was thick and clumpy, without being enough; where everybody, large and small, was cruel; where the boys knew all about the sale, before I got there, and asked me what I had fetched, and who had bought me, and hooted at me, "Going, going, gone!" I never whispered in that wretched place that I had been Haroun, or had had a seraglio – for I knew that if I mentioned my reverses, I should be so worried that I should have to drown myself in the muddy pond near the playground, which looked like the beer.

Ah me, ah me! No other ghost has haunted the boy's room, my friends, since I have occupied it, than the ghost of my own childhood, the ghost of my own innocence, the ghost of my own airy belief. Many a time have I pursued the phantom – never with this man's stride of mine to come up with it, never with these man's hands of mine to touch it, never more to this man's heart of mine to hold it in its purity. And here you see me working out, as cheerfully and thankfully as I may, my doom of shaving in the glass a constant change of customers, and of lying down and rising up with the skeleton allotted to me for my mortal companion.

7

The Ghost in the Garden Room

by Elizabeth Gaskell

M Y FRIEND AND SOLICITOR rubbed his bald forehead – which is quite Shakespearian – with his hand, after a manner he has when I consult him professionally, and took a very large pinch of snuff. "My bedroom," said he, "had been haunted by the ghost of a judge."

"Of a judge?" said all the company.

"Of a judge. In his wig and robes as he sits upon the bench, at assize time. As I have lingered in the great white chair at the side of my fire, when we have all retired for the night to our respective rooms, I have seen and heard him. I never shall forget the description he gave me, and I never have forgotten it since I first heard it."

"Then you have seen and heard him before, Mr Undery?" said my sister.

"Often."

"Consequently, he is not peculiar to this house?"

"By no means. He returns to me in many intervals of quiet leisure, and his story haunts me."

We one and all called for the story, that it might haunt us likewise.

"It fell within the range of his judicial experience," said my friend and solicitor, "and this was the judge's manner of summing it up."

Those words did not apply, of course, to the great pinch of snuff that followed them, but to the words that followed the great pinch of snuff. They were these:

Not many years after the beginning of this century, a worthy couple of the name of Huntroyd occupied a small farm in the North Riding of Yorkshire. They had married late in life, although they were very young when they first began to "keep company" with each other. Nathan Huntroyd had been farm servant to Hester Rose's father, and had made up to her at a time when her parents thought she might do better, and so, without much consultation of her feelings, they had dismissed Nathan in somewhat cavalier fashion. He had drifted far away from his former connections, when an uncle of his died, leaving Nathan – by this time upwards of forty years of age – enough money to stock a small farm and yet to have something over put in the bank against bad times. One of the consequences of this bequest was that Nathan was looking out for a wife and housekeeper in a kind of discreet and leisurely way, when, one day, he heard that his old love, Hester, was not married and flourishing as he had always supposed her to be, but a poor maid-of-all-work, in the town of Ripon. For her father had had a succession of misfortunes, which had brought him in his old age to the workhouse; her mother was dead; her only brother struggling to bring up a large family; and Hester herself a hard-working, homely-looking (at thirty-seven) servant. Nathan had a kind of growling satisfaction (which only lasted for a minute or two, however) in hearing of these turns of Fortune's wheel. He did not make many intelligible remarks to his informant, and to no one else did he say a word. But a few days afterwards, he presented himself, dressed in his Sunday best, at Mrs Thompson's back door in Ripon.

Hester stood there in answer to the good sound knock his good sound oak stick made, she with the light full upon her, he in shadow. For a moment there was silence. He was scanning the face and figure of his old love, for twenty years unseen. The comely beauty of youth had faded away entirely; she was, as I have said, homely-looking, plain-featured, but with a clean skin and pleasant, frank eyes. Her figure was no longer round, but tidily draped in a blue-and-white bedgown, tied round her waist by her white apron strings, and her short red linsey petticoat showed her tidy feet and ankles. Her former love fell into no ecstasies. He simply said to himself, "She'll do," and forthwith began upon his business.

"Hester, thou dost not mind me. I am Nathan, as thy father turned off at a minute's notice, for thinking of thee for a wife, twenty year come Michaelmas next. I have not thought much upon matrimony since. But Uncle Ben has died, leaving me a small matter in the bank, and I have taken Nab End Farm, and put in a bit of stock, and shall want a missus to see after it. Wilt like to come? I'll not mislead thee. It's dairy, and it might have been arable. But arable takes more horses than it suited me to buy, and I'd the offer of a tidy lot of kine. That's all. If thou'lt have me, I'll come for thee as soon as the hay is gotten in."

Hester only said, "Come in, and sit thee down."

He came in, and sat down. For a time she took no more notice of him than of his stick, bustling about to get dinner ready for the family whom she served. He meanwhile watched her brisk, sharp movements, and repeated to himself, "She'll do!" After about twenty minutes of silence thus employed, he got up, saying:

"Well, Hester, I'm going. When shall I come back again?"

"Please thysel', and thou'lt please me," said Hester, in a tone that she tried to make light and indifferent, but he saw that her colour came and went, and that she trembled while she moved about. In another moment Hester was soundly kissed, but when she looked round to scold the middle-aged farmer, he appeared so entirely composed that she hesitated. He said:

"I have pleased mysel', and thee too, I hope. Is it a month's wage, and a month's warning? Today is the eighth. July eighth is our wedding day. I have no time to spend a-wooing before then, and wedding must na take long. Two days is enough to throw away at our time o' life."

It was like a dream, but Hester resolved not to think more about it till her work was done. And when all was cleaned up for the evening, she went and gave her mistress warning, telling her all the history of her life in a very few words. That day month she was married from Mrs Thompson's house.

The issue of the marriage was one boy, Benjamin. A few years after his birth, Hester's brother died at Leeds, leaving ten or twelve children. Hester sorrowed bitterly over this loss, and Nathan showed her much quiet sympathy, although he could not but remember that Jack Rose had added insult to the bitterness of his youth. He helped his wife to make ready to go by the wagon to Leeds. He made light of the household difficulties which came thronging into her mind after all was fixed for her departure. He filled her purse, that she might have wherewithal to alleviate the immediate wants of her brother's family. And as she was leaving, he ran after the wagon. "Stop, stop!" he cried. "Hetty, if thou wilt – if it wunnot be too much for thee – bring back one of Jack's wenches for company, like. We've enough and to spare, and a lass will make the house winsome, as a man may say."

The wagon moved on, while Hester had such a silent swelling of gratitude in her heart, as was both thanks to her husband and thanksgiving to God.

And that was the way that little Bessy Rose came to be an inmate of the Nab End Farm.

Virtue met with its own reward in this instance, and in a clear and tangible shape, too, which need not delude people in general into thinking that such is the usual nature of virtue's rewards. Bessy grew up a bright, affectionate, active girl – a daily comfort to her uncle and aunt. She was so much a darling in the household that they even thought her worthy of their only son Benjamin, who was perfection in their eyes. It is not often the case that two plain, homely people have a child of uncommon beauty, but it is sometimes, and Benjamin Huntroyd was one of these exceptional cases. The hard-working, labour and care-marked farmer, and the mother, who could never have been more than tolerably comely in her best days, produced a son who might have been an earl's son for grace and beauty. Even the hunting squires of the neighbourhood reined up their horses to admire him, as he opened the gates for them. He had no shyness, he was so accustomed to admiration from strangers, and adoration from his parents from his earliest years. As for Bessy Rose, he ruled imperiously over her heart from the time she first set eyes on him. And as she grew older, she grew on in loving, persuading herself that what her uncle and aunt loved so dearly it was her duty to love dearest of all. At every unconscious symptom of the young girl's love for her cousin, his parents smiled and winked: all was going on as they wished, no need to go far afield for Benjamin's wife. The household could go on as it was now; Nathan and Hester sinking into the rest of years, and relinquishing care and authority to those dear ones, who, in the process of time, might bring other ones to share their love.

But Benjamin took it all very coolly. He had been sent to a day school in the neighbouring town – a grammar school, in the high state of neglect in which the majority of such schools were thirty years ago. Neither his father nor his mother knew much of learning. All that they knew (and that directed their choice of a school) was that they could not, by any possibility, part with their darling to a boarding school, that some schooling he must have, and that Squire Pollard's son went to Highminster Grammar School. Squire Pollard's son, and many another son destined to make his parents' hearts ache, went to this school. If it had not been so utterly bad a place of education, the simple farmer and wife might have found it out sooner. But not only did the pupils there learn vice, they also learnt deceit. Benjamin was naturally too clever to remain a dunce, or else, if he had chosen so to be, there was nothing in Highminster Grammar School to hinder his being a dunce of the first water. But to all appearance he grew clever and gentlemanlike. His father and mother were even proud of his airs and graces when he came home for the holidays, taking them for proofs of his refinement, although the practical effect of such refinement was to make him express his contempt for his parents' homely ways and simple ignorance. By the time he was eighteen – an articled clerk in an attorney's office at Highminster, for he had quite declined becoming a "mere clod-hopper", that is to say a hard-working, honest farmer like his father – Bessy Rose was the only person who was dissatisfied with him. The little girl of fourteen instinctively felt there was something wrong about him. Alas! two years more, and the girl of sixteen worshipped his very shadow, and would not see that aught could be wrong with one so soft-spoken, so handsome, so kind as Cousin Benjamin. For Benjamin had found out that the way to cajole his parents out of money for every indulgence he fancied was to pretend to forward their innocent scheme, and make love to his pretty cousin Bessy Rose. He cared just enough for her to make this work of necessity not disagreeable at the time he was performing it. But he found it tiresome to remember her little claims upon him when she was no longer present. The letters he had promised her during his weekly absences at Highminster, the trifling commissions she had asked him to do for her, were all considered in the light of troubles, and even when he was with her, he resented the enquiries she made as to his mode of passing his time, or what female acquaintances he had in Highminster.

When his apprenticeship was ended, nothing would serve him but that he must go up to London for a year or two. Poor Farmer Huntroyd was beginning to repent of his ambition of making his son Benjamin a gentleman. But it was too late to repine now. Both father and mother felt this and, however sorrowful they might be, they were silent, neither demurring nor assenting to Benjamin's proposition when he first made it. But Bessy, through her tears, noticed that both her uncle and aunt seemed unusually tired that night, and sat hand in hand on the fireside settle, idly gazing into the bright flames as if they saw in it pictures of what they had once hoped their lives would have been. Bessy rattled about among the supper things as she put them away after Benjamin's departure, making more noise than usual – as if noise and bustle was what she needed to keep her from bursting out crying – and, having at one keen glance taken in the position and looks of Nathan and Hester, she avoided looking in that direction again, for fear the sight of their wistful faces should make her own tears overflow.

"Sit thee down lass – sit thee down. Bring the creepie stool to the fireside, and let's have a bit of talk over the lad's plans," said Nathan, at last, rousing himself to speak. Bessy came and sat down in front of the fire, and threw her apron over her face, as she rested her head on both hands. Nathan felt as if it was a chance which of the two women burst out crying first. So he thought he would speak, in hopes of keeping off the infection of tears.

"Didst ever hear of this mad plan afore, Bessy?"

"No, never!" Her voice came muffled, and changed from under her apron. Hester felt as if the tone, both of question and answer, implied blame, and this she could not bear.

"We should ha' looked to it when we bound him, for of necessity it would ha' come to this. There's examins, and catechizes, and I dunno what all for him to be put through in London. It's not his fault."

"Which on us said it were?" asked Nathan, rather put out. "Thof, for that matter, a few weeks would carry him over the mire, and make him as good a lawyer as any judge among 'em. Oud Lawson the attorney told me that, in a talk I had wi' him a bit sin. Na, na! It's the lad's own hankering after London that makes him want for to stay there for a year, let alone two."

Nathan shook his head.

"And if it be his own hankering," said Bessy, putting down her apron, her face all aflame, and her eyes swollen up, "I dunnot see harm in it. Lads aren't like lasses, to be teed to their own fireside like th' crook yonder. It's fitting for a young man to go abroad, and see the world afore he settles down."

Hester's hand sought Bessy's, and the two women sat in sympathetic defiance of any blame that should be thrown on the beloved absent. Nathan only said:

"Nay, wench, dunna wax up so; whatten's done, 's done, and worse, it's my doing. I mun needs make my bairn a gentleman, and we mun pay for it."

"Dear Uncle! He wunna spend much, I'll answer for it, and I'll scrimp and save i' th' house to make it good."

"Wench!" said Nathan solemnly. "It were not paying in cash I were speaking on: it were paying in heart's care, and heaviness of soul. Lunnon is a place where the Devil keeps court as well as King George, and my poor chap has more nor once welly fallen into his clutches here. I dunno what he'll do when he gets close within sniff of him."

"Don't let him go, Father!" said Hester, for the first time taking this view. Hitherto she had only thought of her own grief at parting with him. "Father, if you think so, keep him here, safe under our own eye."

"Nay!" said Nathan. "He's past time o' life for that. Why, there's not one on us knows where he is at this present time, and he not gone out of sight an hour. He's too big to be put back i' th' go-kart, Mother, or kept within doors with the chair turned bottom upwards."

"I wish he were a wee bairn lying in my arms again. It were a sore day when I weaned him, and I think life's been gotten sorer and sorer at every turn he's ta'en towards manhood."

"Coom, lass, that's noan the way to be talking. Be thankful to Marcy that thou'st getten a man for the son as stands five foot eleven in's stockings, and ne'er a sick piece about him. We wunnot grudge him his fling, will we, Bess, my wench. He'll be coming back in a year, or mebby a bit more, and be a' for settling in a quiet town like, wi' a wife that's noan so fur fra' me at this very minute. An' we oud folk, as we get into years, must gi' up farm, and tak a bit on a house near Lawyer Benjamin."

And so the good Nathan, his own heart heavy enough, tried to soothe his womenkind. But of the three, his eyes were longest in closing, his apprehensions the deepest founded.

"I misdoubt me I hanna done well by th' lad. I misdoubt me sore," was the thought that kept him awake till day began to dawn. "Summet's wrong about him, or folk would na look at me wi' such piteous-like een when they speak on him. I can see th' meaning of it, thof I'm too proud to let on. And Lawson, too, he holds his tongue more nor he should do, when I ax him how my lad's getting on, and whatten sort of a lawyer he'll mak. God be marciful to Hester an' me, if th' lad's gone away! God be marciful! But mebby it's this lying waking a' the night through that maks me so fearfu'. Why, when I were his age, I daur be bound I shoul ha' spent money fast enoof, i' I could ha' come by it. But I had to arm it; that makes a great differ'. Well! It were hard to thwart th' child of our old age, and we waiten so long for to have 'un!"

Next morning Nathan rode Moggy the cart horse into Highminster to see Mr Lawson. Anybody who saw him ride out of his own yard would have been struck with the change in him when he returned – a change which more than a day's unusual exercise should have made in a man of his years. He scarcely held the reins at all. One jerk of Moggy's head would have plucked them out of his hands. His head was bent forwards, his eyes looking on some unseen thing, with long unwinking gaze. But as he drew near home on his return, he made an effort to recover himself.

"No need fretting them," he said, "lads will be lads. But I didna think he had it in him to be so thowtless, young as he is. Well, well! He'll mebby get more wisdom i' Lunnon. Anyways it's best to cut him off fra such evil lads as Will Hawker, and suchlike. It's they as have led my boy astray. He were a good chap till he knowed them – a good chap till he knowed them."

But he put all his cares in the background when he came into the house place, where both Bessy and his wife met him at the door, and both would fain lend a hand to take off his greatcoat.

"Theer, wenches, theer! Ye might let alone for to get out on's clothes! Why, I might ha' struck thee, lass." And he went on talking, trying to keep them off for a time from the subject that all had at heart. But there was no putting them off for ever, and, by dint of repeated questioning on his wife's part, more was got out than he had ever meant to tell – enough to grieve both his hearers sorely, and yet the brave old man still kept the worst in his own breast.

The next day Benjamin came home for a week or two before making his great start to London. His father kept him at a distance, and was solemn and quiet in his manner to the young man. Bessy, who had shown anger enough at first, and had uttered many a sharp speech, began to relent, and then to feel hurt and displeased that her uncle should persevere so long in his cold, reserved manner, and Benjamin just going to leave them. Her aunt went, tremblingly busy, about the clothes presses and drawers, as if afraid of letting herself think either of the past or the future; only once or twice, coming behind her son, she suddenly stooped over his sitting figure, and kissed his cheek, and stroked his hair. Bessy remembered afterwards – long years afterwards – how he had tossed his head away with nervous irritability on one of these occasions, and had muttered – her aunt did not hear it, but Bessy did:

"Can't you leave a man alone?"

Towards Bessy herself he was pretty gracious. No other words express his manner: it was not warm, nor tender, nor cousinly, but there was an assumption of underbred politeness towards her as a young, pretty woman; which politeness was neglected in his authoritative or grumbling manner towards his mother, or his sullen silence before his father. He once or twice ventured on a compliment to Bessy on her personal appearance. She stood still, and looked at him with astonishment.

"How's my eyes changed sin last thou sawst them," she asked, "that thou must be telling me about 'em i' that fashion? I'd rayther by a deal see thee helping the mother when she's dropped her knitting needle and canna see i' th' dusk for to pick it up."

But Bessy thought of his pretty speech about her eyes long after he had forgotten making it, and would have been puzzled to tell the colour of them. Many a day, after he was gone, did she look earnestly in the little oblong looking glass which hung up against the wall of her little sleeping chamber, but which she used to take down in order to examine the eyes he had praised, murmuring to herself, "Pretty soft grey eyes! Pretty soft grey eyes!" until she would hang up the glass again with a sudden laugh and a rosy blush.

In the days when he had gone away to the vague distance and vaguer place – the city called London – Bessy tried to forget all that had gone against her feeling of the affection and duty that a son owed to his parents, and she had many things to forget of this kind that would keep surging up into her mind. For instance, she wished that he had not objected to the homespun, home-made shirts which his mother and she had had such pleasure in getting ready for him. He might not know, it was true – and so her love urged – how carefully and evenly the thread had been spun: how, not content with bleaching the yarn in the sunniest meadow, the linen, on its return from the weaver's, had been spread out afresh on the sweet summer grass, and watered carefully night after night when there was no dew to perform the kindly office. He did not know – for no one but Bessy herself did – how many false or large stitches, made large and false by her aunt's failing eyes (who yet liked to do the choicest part of the stitching all by herself), Bessy had unpicked at night in her own room, and with dainty fingers had restitched, sewing eagerly in the dead of night. All this he did not know, or he could never have complained of the coarse texture, the old-fashioned make of these shirts, and urged on his mother to give him part of her little store of egg and butter money in order to buy newer-fashioned linen in Highminster.

When once that little precious store of his mother's was discovered, it was well for Bessy's peace of mind that she did not know how loosely her aunt counted up the coins, mistaking guineas for shillings, or just the other way, so that the amount was seldom the same in the old black spoutless teapot. Yet this son, this hope, this love, had yet a strange power of fascination over the household. The evening before he left, he sat between his parents, a hand in theirs on either side, and Bessy on the old creepie stool, her head lying on her aunt's knee, and looking up at him from time to time, as if to learn his face off by heart, till his glances, meeting hers, made her drop her eyes, and only sigh.

He stopped up late that night with his father, long after the women had gone to bed. But not to sleep, for I will answer for it the grey-haired mother never slept a wink till the late dawn of the autumn day, and Bessy heard her uncle come upstairs with heavy, deliberate footsteps, and go to the old stocking which served him for bank, and count out golden guineas – once he stopped, but again he went on afresh, as if resolved to crown his gift with liberality. Another long pause – in which she could but indistinctly hear continued words, it might have been advice, it might be a prayer, for it was in her uncle's voice, and then father and son came up to bed. Bessy's room was but parted from her cousin's by a thin wooden partition, and the last sound she distinctly heard, before her eyes, tired out with crying, closed themselves in sleep, was the guineas clinking down upon each other at regular intervals, as if Benjamin were playing at pitch and toss with his father's present.

After he was gone, Bessy wished he had asked her to walk part of the way with him into Highminster. She was all ready, her things laid out on the bed, but she could not accompany him without invitation.

The little household tried to close over the gap as best they might. They seemed to set themselves to their daily work with unusual vigour, but somehow when evening came, there had been little done. Heavy hearts never make light work, and there was no telling how much care and anxiety each had had to bear in secret in the field, at the wheel or in the dairy. Formerly he was looked for every Saturday; looked for, though he might not come, or if he came, there were things to be spoken about that made his visit anything but a pleasure: still he might come, and all things might go right, and then what sunshine, what gladness to those humble people. But now he was away, and dreary winter was come on; old folks' sight fails, and the evenings were long and sad, in spite of all Bessy could do or say. And he did not write so often as he might – so everyone thought; though everyone would have been ready to defend him from either of the others who had expressed such a thought aloud. "Surely!" said Bessy to herself, when the first primroses peeped out in a sheltered and sunny hedge bank, and she gathered them as she passed home from afternoon church. "Surely there never will be such a dreary, miserable winter again as this has been." There had been a great change in Nathan and Bessy Huntroyd during this last year. The spring before, when Benjamin was yet the subject of more hopes than fears, his father and mother looked what I may call an elderly middle-aged couple: people who had a good deal of hearty work in them yet. Now – it was not his absence alone that caused the change – they looked frail and old, as if each day's natural trouble was a burden more than they could bear. For Nathan had heard sad reports about his only child, and had told them solemnly to his wife, as things too bad to be believed, and yet, "God help us if indeed he is such a lad as this!" Their eyes were become too dry and hollow for many tears; they sat together, hand in hand, and shivered, and sighed, and did not speak many words, or dare to look at each other, and then Hester had said:

CHAPTER 7: THE GHOST IN THE GARDEN ROOM BY ELIZABETH GASKELL

"We mauna tell th' lass. Young folks' hearts break wi' a little, and she'd be apt to fancy it were true." Here the old woman's voice broke into a kind of piping cry, but she struggled, and her next words were all right. "We mauna tell her, he's bound to be fond on her, and mebby if she thinks well on him, ane loves him, it will bring him straight."

"God grant it!" said Nathan.

"God shall grant it," said Hester, passionately moaning out her words, and then repeating them – alas! – with a vain repetition.

"It's a bad place for lying, is Highminster," said she, at length, as if impatient of the silence. "I never knowed such a place for getting up stories. But Bessy knows nought on, and nother you nor me belie'es un; that's one blessing."

But if they did not in their hearts believe them, how came they to look so sad and worn, beyond what mere age could do?

Then came round another year, another winter, yet more miserable than the last. This year, with the primroses, came Benjamin; a bad, hard, flippant young man, with yet enough of specious manners and handsome countenance to make his appearance striking at first to those to whom the aspect of a London fast young man of the lowest order is strange and new. Just at first, as he sauntered in with a swagger and an air of indifference, which was partly assumed, partly real, his old parents felt a simple kind of awe of him, as if he were not their son, but a real gentleman, but they had too much fine instinct in their homely natures not to know, after a very few minutes had passed, that this was not a true prince.

"Whatten ever does he mean," said Hester to her niece, as soon as they were alone, "by a' them maks and wearloks? And he minces his words as if his tongue were clipped short, or split like a magpie's. Hech! London is as bad as a hot day i' August for spoiling good flesh, for he were a good-looking lad when he went up, and now, look at him, with his skin gone into lines and flourishes, just like first page on a copybook!"

"I think he looks a deal better, Aunt, for them new-fashioned whiskers!" said Bessy, blushing still at the remembrance of the kiss he had given her on first seeing her – a pledge, she thought, poor girl, that, in spite of his long silence in letter-writing, he still looked upon her as his troth-plight wife. There were things about him which none of them liked, although they never spoke about them, yet there was also something to gratify them all in the way in which he remained quiet at Nab End, instead of seeking variety, as he had formerly done, by constantly stealing off to the neighbouring town. His father had paid all the debts that he knew of soon after Benjamin had gone up to London; so there were no duns that his parents knew to alarm him, and keep him at home. And he went out in the morning with the old man, his father, and lounged by his side, as Nathan went round his fields, with busy yet infirm gait, having heart, as he would have expressed it, in all that was going on, because at length his son seemed to take an interest in all the farming affairs, and stood patiently by his side, while he compared his own small galloways with the great short-horns looming over his neighbour's hedge.

"It's a slovenly way, thou seest, that of selling th' milk; folk don't care whether it's good or not, so that they get their pint-measure full o' stuff that's watered afore it leaves th' beast instead o' honest cheating by the help o' th' pump. But look at Bessy's butter, what skill it shows! Part her own manner of making, and part good choice o' cattle. It's a pleasure to see her basket, a' packed ready for to go to market, and it's noan o' a pleasure for to see the buckets fu' of their blue starch water as yon beasts give. I'm thinking they crossed th' breed wi' a pump, not long sin'. Hech! but our Bessy's a cleaver canny wench! I sometimes think thou'lt be for gi'ing up th'law, and taking to th' oud trade, when thou wedst wi' her!" This was intended to be a skilful way of ascertaining whether there was any ground for the old farmer's wish and prayer that Benjamin might give up the law, and return to the primitive occupation of his father. Nathan dared to hope it now, since his son had never made much by his profession, owing, as he had said, to his want of a connection, and the farm, and the stock, and the clean wife, too, were ready to his hand, and Nathan could safely rely on himself never in his most unguarded moments to reproach his son with the hardly earned hundreds that had been spent on his education. So the old man listened with painful interest to the answer which his son was evidently struggling to make, coughing a little and blowing his nose before he spoke.

"Well! you see, father, law is a precarious livelihood; a man, as I may express myself, has no chance in the profession, unless he is known – known to the judges, and tip-top barristers, and that sort of thing. Now you see my mother and you have no acquaintance that you may exactly call in that line. But luckily I have met with a man, a friend as I may say, who is really a first-rate fellow, knowing everybody, from the Lord Chancellor downwards, and he has offered me a share in his business – a partnership in short…" He hesitated a little.

"I'm sure that's uncommon kind of the gentleman," said Nathan. "I should like for to thank him mysen, for it's not many as would pick up a young chap out o' th' dirt as it were, and say, 'Here's hauf my good fortune for you, sir, and your very good health.' Most on 'em, when they're getting a bit o' luck, run off wi' it to keep it a' to themselves, and gobble it down in a corner. What may be his name, for I should like for to know it?"

"You don't quite apprehend me, Father. A great deal of what you've said is true to the letter. People don't like to share their good luck, as you say."

"The more credit to them as does," broke in Nathan.

"Ay, but you see even such a fine fellow as my friend Cavendish does not like to give away half his good practice for nothing. He expects an equivalent."

"An equivalent," said Nathan; his voice had dropped down an octave. "And what may that be? There's always some meaning in grand words, I take it, though I'm not book-larned enough to find it out."

"Why, in this case the equivalent he demands for taking me into partnership, and afterwards relinquishing the whole business to me, is three hundred pounds down."

Benjamin looked sideways from under his eyes to see how his father took the proposition. His father struck his stick deep down in the ground and, leaning one hand upon it, faced round at him.

"Then thy fine friend may go and be hanged. Three hunder pound! I'll be darned an' danged too, if I know where to get 'em, e'en if I'd be making a fool o' thee an' mysen too."

He was out of breath by this time. His son took his father's first words in dogged silence; it was but the burst of surprise he had led himself to expect, and did not daunt him for long.

"I should think, sir—"

"'Sir' – whatten for dost thou 'sir' me? Is them's your manners? I'm plain Nathan Huntroyd, who never took on to be a gentleman, but I have paid my way up to this time, which I shannot do much longer, if I'm to have a son coming home an' asking me for three hunder pounds, just as if I were a cow, and had nothing to do but let down my milk to the first person as strokes me."

"Well, Father," said Benjamin, with an affectation of frankness, "then there's nothing for me but to do as I have often planned before – go and emigrate."

"And *what*?" said his father, looking sharply and steadily at him.

"Emigrate. Go to America, or India, or some colony, where there would be an opening for a young man of spirit."

Benjamin has reserved this proposition for his trump card, expecting by means of it to carry all before him. But to his surprise his father plucked his stick out of the hole he had made when he so vehemently thrust it into the ground, and he walked on four or five steps in advance; there he stood still again, and there was a dead silence for a few minutes. "It 'ud mebby be th' best thing thou couldst do," the father began. Benjamin set his teeth hard to keep in curses. It was well for poor Nathan he did not look round then, and see the look his son gave him. "But it would come hard like upon us, upon Hester and me, for, whether thou'rt a good 'un or not, thou'rt our flesh and blood, our only bairn, and if thou'rt not all as a man could wish it's mebby been the fault on our pride i' thee. It 'ud kill the missus if he went off to Amerikay, and Bess, too, the lass as thinks so much on him." The speech originally addressed to his son had wandered off into a monologue – as keenly listened to by Benjamin, however, as if it had been spoken to him. After a pause of consideration his father turned round. "Yon man – I wunnot call him a friend o' yourn, to think of asking you for such a mint o' money – is not th' only one, I'll be bound, as could give ye a start i' th' law? Other folks 'ud, mebby, do it for less?"

"Not one of 'em, to give me equal advantages," said Benjamin, thinking he perceived signs of relenting.

"Well, then, thou mayst tell him that it's neither he nor thee as'll see th' sight o' three hunder pound o' my money. I'll not deny as I've a bit laid up again a rainy day; it's not so much as thatten though, and a part on it is for Bessy, as has been like a daughter to us."

"But Bessy is to be your real daughter some day, when I've a home to take her to," said Benjamin, for he played very fast and loose, even in his own mind, with his engagement with Bessy. Present with her, when she was looking her brightest and best, he behaved to her as if they were engaged lovers; absent from her, he looked upon her rather as a good wedge, to be driven into his parent's favour on his behalf. Now, however, he was not exactly untrue in speaking as if he meant to make her his wife, for the thought was in his mind, though he made use of it to work upon his father.

"It will be a dree day for us, then," said the old man. "But God'll have us in his keeping, and 'll mebby be taking more care on us i' heaven by that time than Bess, good lass as she is, has had on us at Nab End. Her heart is set on thee, too. But, lad, I hanna gotten the three hunder; I keeps my cash i' th' stocking, thou knowst, till it reaches fifty pound, and then I takes it to Ripon Bank. Now the last scratch they're gi'en me made it just two hunder, and I hanna but on to fifteen pound yet i' the stockin', and I meant one hunder an' the red cow's calf to be for Bess, she's ta'en such pleasure like i' rearing it."

Benjamin gave a sharp glance at his father to see if he was telling the truth, and that a suspicion of the old man, his father, had entered into his son's head, tells enough of his own character.

"I canna do it – I canna do it, for sure – although I shall like it to think as I had helped on the wedding. There's the black heifer to be sold yet, and she'll fetch a matter of ten pound, but a deal on't will be needed for seed corn, for the arable did but bad last year, and I thought I would try – I'll tell thee what, lad! I'll make it as though Bess lent thee her hunder, only thou must give her a writ of hand for it, and thou shalt have a' the money i' Ripon Bank, and see if the lawyer wunnot let thee have a share of what he offered thee for three hunder, for two. I dunnot mean for to wrong him, but thou must get a fair share for the money. At times I think thou'rt done by folk; now, I wadna have you cheat a bairn of a brass farthing; same time I wadna have thee so soft as to be cheated."

To explain this, it should be told that some of the bills which Benjamin had received money from his father to pay had been altered so as to include other and less creditable expenses which the young man had incurred, and the simple old farmer, who had still much faith left in him for his boy, was acute enough to perceive that he had paid above the usual price for the articles he had purchased.

After some hesitation, Benjamin agreed to receive this two hundred, and promised to employ it to the best advantage in setting himself up in business. He had, nevertheless, a strange hankering after the additional fifteen pounds that was left to accumulate in the stocking. It was his, he thought, as heir to his father, and he soon lost some of his usual complaisance for Bessy that evening, as he dwelt on the idea that there was money being laid by for her, and grudged it to her even in imagination. He thought more of this fifteen pound that he was not to have, than of all the hardly earned and humbly saved two hundred that he was to come into possession of. Meanwhile Nathan was in unusual spirits that evening. He was so generous and affectionate at heart that he had an unconscious satisfaction in having helped two people on the road to happiness by the sacrifice of the greater part of his property. The very fact of having trusted his son so largely seemed to make Benjamin more worthy of trust in his father's estimation. The sole idea he tried to banish was that, if all came to pass as he hoped, both Benjamin and Bessy would be settled far away from Nab End, but then he had a childlike reliance that "God would take care of him and his missus somehow or anodder. It wur o' no use looking too far ahead."

Bessy had to hear many unintelligible jokes from her uncle that night, for he made no doubt that Benjamin had told her all that had passed, whereas the truth was his son had said never a word to his cousin on the subject.

When the old couple were in bed, Nathan told his wife of the promise he had made to his son, and the plan in life which the advance of the two hundred was to promote. Poor Hester was a little startled at the sudden change in the destination of the sum, which she had long thought of with secret pride as "money i'th'bank". But she was willing enough to part with it, if necessary, for Benjamin. Only how such a sum could be necessary was the puzzle. But even this perplexity was jostled out of her mind by the overwhelming idea, not only of "our Ben" settling in London, but of Bessy going there too as his wife. This great trouble swallowed up all care about money, and Hester shivered all the night through with distress. In the morning, as Bessy was kneading the bread, her aunt, who had been sitting by the fire in an unusual manner for one of her active habits, said:

"I reckon we mun go th' shop for our bread, an' that's a thing I never thought to come to so long as I lived."

Bessy looked up from her kneading, surprised.

"I'm sure I'm noan going to eat their nasty stuff. What for do ye want to get baker's bread, Aunt? This dough will rise as high as a kite in a south wind."

"I'm not up to kneading as I could do once; it welly breaks my back, and when thou'rt off in London, I reckon we mun buy our bread, first time in my life."

"I'm not a-going to London," said Bessy, kneading away with fresh resolution, and growing very red, either with the idea or the exertion.

"But our Ben is going partner wi' a great London lawyer, and thou know'st well he'll not tarry long but what he'll fetch thee."

"Now, Aunt," said Bessy, stripping her arms of the dough, but still not looking up, "if that's all, don't fret yourself. Ben will have twenty minds in his head afore he settles, eyther in business or in wedlock. I sometimes wonder," she said, with increasing vehemence, "why I go on thinking on him, for I dunnot think he thinks on me when I'm out o' sight. I've a month's mind to try and forget him this time when he leaves us – that I have!"

"For a shame, wench! And he to be planning and purposing all for thy sake. It wur only yesterday as he wur talking to thy uncle, and mapping it out so clever; only thou seest, wench, it'll be dree work for us when both thee and him is gone."

The old woman began to cry the kind of tearless cry of the aged. Bessy hastened to comfort her, and the two talked, and grieved, and hoped, and planned for the days that now were to be, till they ended, the one in being consoled, the other in being secretly happy.

Nathan and his son came back from Highminster that evening, with their business transacted in the roundabout way, which was most satisfactory to the old man. If he had thought it necessary to take half as much pains in ascertaining the truth of the plausible details by which his son bore out the story of the offered partnership, as he did in trying to get his money conveyed to London in the most secure manner, it would have been well for him. But he knew nothing of all this, and acted in the way which satisfied his anxiety best. He came home tired, but content, not in such high spirits as on the night before, but as easy in his mind as he could be on the eve of his son's departure. Bessy, pleasantly agitated by her aunt's tale of the morning of her cousin's true love for her – what ardently we wish we long believe – and the plan which was to end in their marriage – end to her, the woman, at least – Bessy looked almost pretty in her bright, blushing comeliness, and more than once, as she moved about from kitchen to dairy, Benjamin pulled her towards him, and gave her a kiss. To all such proceedings the old couple were wilfully blind, and, as night drew on, everyone became sadder and quieter, thinking of the parting that was to be on the morrow. As the hours drew on, Bessy, too, became subdued, and, by and by, her simple cunning was exerted to get Benjamin to sit down next his mother, whose very heart was yearning after him, as Bessy saw. When once her child was placed by her side, and she had got possession of his hand, the old woman kept stroking it, and murmuring long unused words of endearment, such as she had spoken to him while he was yet a little child. But all this was wearisome to him. As long as he might play with, and plague, and caress Bessy, he had not been sleepy, but now he yawned loudly. Bessy could have boxed his ears for not curbing this gaping; at any rate, he needed not to have done it so openly – so almost ostentatiously. His mother was more pitiful.

"Thou'rt tired, my lad!" said she, putting her hand fondly on his shoulder, but it fell off as he stood up suddenly and said:

"Yes, deuced tired! I'm off to bed." And with a rough careless kiss all round, even to Bessy, as if he was "deuced tired" of playing the lover, he was gone, leaving the three to gather up their thoughts slowly, and follow him upstairs.

He seemed almost impatient at them for rising betimes to see him off the next morning, and made no more of a goodbye than some such speech as this: "Well, good folk, when next I see you, I hope you'll have merrier faces than you have today. Why, you might be going to a funeral; it's enough to scare a man from the place; you look quite ugly to what you did last night, Bess."

He was gone, and they turned into the house, and settled to the long day's work without many words about their loss. They had no time for unnecessary talking, indeed, for much had been left undone during his short visit that ought to have been done, and they had now to work double tides. Hard work was their comfort for many a long day.

For some time, Benjamin's letters, if not frequent, were full of exultant accounts of his well-doing. It is true that the details of his prosperity were somewhat vague, but the fact was broadly and unmistakably stated. Then came longer pauses, shorter letters, altered in tone. About a year after he had left them, Nathan received a letter, which bewildered and irritated him exceedingly. Something had gone wrong – what, Benjamin did not say – but the letter ended with a request that was almost a demand, for the remainder of his father's savings, whether in the stocking or the bank. Now the year had not been prosperous with Nathan; there had been an epidemic among cattle, and he had suffered along with his neighbours, and, moreover, the price of cows, when he had bought some to repair his wasted stock, was higher than he had ever remembered it before. The fifteen pounds in the stocking, which Benjamin left, had diminished to little more than three, and to have that required of him in so peremptory a manner! Before Nathan imparted the contents of this letter to anyone (Bessy and her aunt had gone to market on a neighbour's cart that day), he got pen and ink and paper, and wrote back an ill-spelt, but very implicit and stern negative. Benjamin had had his portion, and if he could not make it do, so much the worse for him; his father had no more to give him. That was the substance of the letter.

The letter was written, directed and sealed, and given to the country postman, returning to Highminster after his day's distribution and collection of letters, before Hester and Bessy returned from market. It had been a pleasant day of neighbourly meeting and sociable gossip: prices had been high, and they were in good spirits, only agreeably tired, and full of small pieces of news. It was some time before they found out how flatly all their talk fell on the ears of the stay-at-home listener. But when they saw that his depression was caused by something beyond their powers of accounting for by any little everyday cause, they urged him to tell them what was the matter. His anger had not gone off. It had rather increased by dwelling upon it, and he spoke it out in good resolute terms, and, long ere he had ended, the two women were as sad, if not as angry, as himself. Indeed, it was many days before either feeling wore away in the minds of those who entertained them. Bessy was the soonest comforted, because she found a vent for her sorrow in action; an action that was half as a kind of compensation for many a sharp word that she had spoken when her cousin had done anything to displease her on his last visit, and half because she believed that he never could have written such a letter to his father unless his want of money had been very pressing and real; though how he could ever have wanted money so soon, after such a heap of it had been given to him, was more than she could justly say. Bessy got out all her savings of little presents of sixpences and shillings, ever since she had been a child, of all the money she had gained for the eggs of two hens, called her own, she put all together, and it was above two pound – two pound five and sevenpence, to speak accurately – and, leaving out the penny as a nest egg for her future savings, she put up the rest in a little parcel, and sent it, with a note, to Benjamin's address in London:

From a well-wisher.
DR BENJAMIN, Unkle has lost 2 cows and a vast of monney. He is a good deal Angored, but more Troubled. So no more at present. Hopeing this will finding you well as it leaves us. Tho' lost to Site, To Memory Dear. Repayment not kneeded.

Your effectonet cousin,
Elizabeth Rose

When this packet was once fairly sent off, Bessy began to sing again over her work. She never expected the mere form of acknowledgment; indeed, she had such faith in the carrier (who took parcels to York, whence they were forwarded to London by coach), that she felt sure that he would go on purpose to London to deliver anything entrusted to him, if he had not full confidence in the person, persons, coach and horses to whom he committed it. Therefore she was not anxious that she did not hear of its arrival. "Giving a thing to a man as one knows," said she herself, "is a vast different to poking a thing through a hole into a box, th'inside of which one has never clapped eyes on, and yet letters get safe some ways or another." (This belief in the infallibility of the post was destined a shock before long.) But she had a secret yearning for Benjamin's thanks, and some of the old words of love that she had been without so long. Nay, she even thought – when day after day, week after week, passed by without a line – that he might be winding up his affairs in that weary, wasteful London, and coming back to Nab End to thank her in person.

One day – her aunt was upstairs, inspecting the summer's make of cheeses, her uncle out in the fields – the postman brought a letter into the kitchen to Bessy. A country postman, even now, is not much pressed for time, and in those days there were but few letters to distribute, and they were only sent out from Highminster once a week into the district in which Nab End was situated, and on those occasions the letter carrier usually paid morning calls on the various people for whom he had letters. So, half standing by the dresser, half sitting on it, he began to rummage out his bag. "It's a queer-like thing I've got for Nathan this time. I am afraid it will bear ill news in it, for there's 'Dead Letter Office' stamped on the top of it."

"Lord save us!" said Bessy, and sat down on the nearest chair, as white as a sheet. In an instant, however, she was up, and, snatching the ominous letter out of the man's hands, she pushed him before her out of the house, and said, "Be off wi' thee, afore Aunt comes down," and ran past him as hard as she could, till she reached the field where she expected to find her uncle.

"Uncle," said she, breathless, "what is it? Oh, Uncle, speak! Is he dead?"

Nathan's hands trembled, and his eyes dazzled. "Take it," he said, "and tell me what it is."

"It's a letter – it's from you to Benjamin, it is – and there's words printed with it, 'Not known at the address given'; so they've sent it back to the writer – that's you, Uncle. Oh, it gave me such a start, with them nasty words printed outside!"

Nathan had taken the letter back into his own hands, and was turning it over, while he strove to understand what the quick-witted Bessy had picked up at a glance. But he arrived at a different conclusion.

"He's dead?" said he. "The lad is dead, and he never knowed how as I were sorry I wrote to 'un so sharp. My lad! My lad!" Nathan sat down on the ground where he stood, and covered his face with his old, withered hands. The letter returned to him was one which he had written with infinite pains and at various times, to tell his child, in kinder words and at greater length than he had done before, the reasons why he could not send him the money demanded. And now Benjamin was dead; nay, the old man immediately jumped to the conclusion that his child had been starved to death, without money, in a wild, wide, strange place. All he could say at first was:

"My heart, Bess – my heart is broken!" And he put his hand to his side, still keeping his shut eyes covered with the other, as though he never wished to see the light of day again. Bessy was down by his side in an instant, holding him in her arms, chafing and kissing him.

"It's noan so bad, Uncle; he's not dead; the letter does not say that, dunnot think it. He's flitted from that lodging, and the lazy tyke dunna know where to find him, and so they just send y' back th' letter, instead of trying fra' house to house, as Mark Benson would. I've always heerd tell on south country folk for laziness. He's noan dead, Uncle; he's just flitted, and he'll let us know afore long where he's getten to. Mebby it's a cheaper place, for that lawyer has cheated him, ye recklet, and he'll be trying to live for as little as can, that's all, Uncle. Dunnot take on so, for it doesna say he's dead."

By this time, Bessy was crying with agitation, although she firmly believed in her own view of the case, and had felt the opening of the ill-favoured letter as a great relief. Presently she began to urge both with word and action upon her uncle that he should sit no longer on the damp grass. She pulled him up, for he was very stiff, and, as he said, "all shaken to dithers". She made him walk about, repeating over and over again her solution of the case, always in the same words, beginning again and again, "He's noan dead, it's just been a flitting," and so on. Nathan shook his head, and tried to be convinced, but it was a steady belief in his own heart for all that. He looked so deathly ill on his return home with Bessy (for she would not let him go on with his day's work), that his wife made sure he had taken cold, and he, weary and indifferent to life, was glad to subside into bed and the rest from exertion which his real bodily illness gave him. Neither Bessy nor he spoke of the letter again, even to each other, for many days, and Bessy found means to stop Mark Benson's tongue, and satisfy his kindly curiosity by giving him the rosy side of her own view of the case.

Nathan got up again an older man in looks and constitution by ten years for that week of bed. His wife gave him many a scolding on his imprudence for sitting down in the wet field, if ever so tired. But now she, too, was beginning to be uneasy at Benjamin's long-continued silence. She could not write herself, but she urged her husband many a time to send a letter to ask for news of her lad. He said nothing in reply for some time; at length he told her he would write next Sunday afternoon. Sunday was his general time for writing, and this Sunday he meant to go to church for the first time since his illness. On Saturday he was very persistent against his wife's wishes (backed by Bessy as hard as she could), in resolving to go into Highminster to market. The change would do him good, he said. But he came home tired, and a little mysterious in his ways. When he went to the shippon the last thing at night, he asked Bessy to go with him and hold the lantern, while he looked at an ailing cow, and, when they were fairly out of the earshot of the house, he pulled out a little shop parcel and said to her:

"Thou'lt put that on ma Sunday hat, wilt 'ou lass? It'll be a bit on a comfort to me, for I know my lad's dead and gone, though I dunna speak on it for fear o' grieving th' old woman and ye."

"I'll put it on, Uncle, if... But he's noan dead." (Bessy was sobbing.)

"I know – I know, lass. I dunnot wish other folk to hold my opinion, but I'd like to wear a bit o' crape, out o' respect to my boy. It 'ud have done me good for to have ordered a black coat, but she'd see if I had na' on my wedding coat, Sundays, for a' she's losing her eyesight, poor old wench! But she'll ne'er take notice o' a bit o' crape. Thou'll put it on all canny and tidy."

So Nathan went to church with a strip of crape as narrow as Bessy durst venture to make it round his hat. Such is the contradictoriness of human nature that, though he was most anxious his wife should not hear of his conviction that their son was dead, he was half hurt that none of the neighbours noticed his sign of mourning so far as to ask him for whom he wore it.

But after a while, when they never heard a word from or about Benjamin, the household wonder as to what had become of him grew so painful and strong that Nathan no longer kept his idea to himself. Poor Hester, however, rejected it with her whole will, heart and soul. She could not and would not believe – nothing should make her believe – that her only child Benjamin had died without some sign of love or farewell to her. No arguments could shake her in this. She believed that if all natural means of communication between her and him had been cut off at the last supreme moment – if death had come upon him in an instant, sudden and unexpected – her intense love would, she believed, have been supernaturally made conscious of the blank. Nathan at times tried to feel glad that she could still hope to see the lad again, but at other moments he wanted her sympathy in his grief, his self-reproach, his weary wonder as to how and what they had done wrong in the treatment of their son, that he had been such a care and sorrow to his parents. Bessy was convinced, first by her aunt, and then by her uncle

– honestly convinced – on both sides of the argument, and so for the time able to sympathize with each. But she lost her youth in a very few months; she looked set and middle-aged long before she ought to have done, and rarely smiled and never sang again.

All sorts of new arrangements were required by the blow which told so miserably upon the energies of all the household at Nab End. Nathan could no longer go about and direct his two men, taking a good turn of work himself at busy times. Hester lost her interest in her dairy, for which indeed her increasing loss of sight unfitted her. Bessy would either do fieldwork, or attend to the cows, the shippon, or churn, or make cheese; she did all well, no longer merrily, but with something of stern cleverness. But she was not sorry when her uncle one evening told her aunt and her that a neighbouring farmer, Job Kirkby, had made him an offer to take so much of his land off his hands as would leave him only pasture enough for two cows, and no arable to attend to; while Farmer Kirkby did not wish to interfere with anything in the house, only would be glad to use some of the outbuildings for his fattening cattle.

"We can do wi' Hawky and Daisy; it'll leave us eight or ten pound o' butter to take to market i' summertime, and keep us fra' thinking too much, which is what I'm dreading on as I get into years."

"Ay," said his wife. "Thou'll not have to go so far afield, if it's only the Aster Toft as is on thy hands. And Bess will have to gi' up her pride i' cheese, and tak' to making cream butter. I'd allays a fancy for trying at cream butter, but th' whey had to be used; else, where I come fra, they'd never ha' looked near whey butter."

When Hester was left alone with Bessy, she said, in allusion to this change of plan:

"I'm thankful to the Lord as it is: for I were allays feared Nathan would have to gie up the house and farm altogether, and then the lad would na' know where to find us when he came back fra Merikay. He's gone there to make his fortune, I'll be bound. Keep up thy heart, lass, he'll be home some day, and have sown his wild oats. Eh! but thatten's a pretty story i' the Gospels about the Prodigal who'd to eat the pigs' vittle at one time, but ended i' clover in his father's house. And I'm sure our Nathan'll be ready to forgive him, and love him, and make much of him, mebby a deal more nor me, who never gave in to 's death. It'll be liken to a resurrection to our Nathan."

Farmer Kirkby then took by far the greater part of the land belonging to Nab End Farm, and the work about the rest, and about the two remaining cows, was easily done by three pairs of willing hands with a little occasional assistance. The Kirkby family were pleasant enough to have a deal with. There was a son, a stiff, grave bachelor, who was very particular and methodical about his work, and rarely spoke to anyone. But Nathan took it into his head that John Kirkby was looking after Bessy, and was a good deal troubled in his mind in consequence, for it was the first time he had to face the effects of his belief in his son's death, and he discovered to his own surprise that he had not that implicit faith which would make it easy for him to look upon Bessy as the wife of another man than the one to whom she had been betrothed in her youth. As, however, John Kirkby seemed in no hurry to make his intentions (if indeed he had any) clear to Bessy, it was only at times that this jealousy on behalf of his lost son seized upon Nathan.

But people, old, and in deep hopeless sorrow, grow irritable at times, however they may repent and struggle against their irritability. There were days when Bessy had to bear a good deal from her uncle, but she loved him so dearly and respected him so much that, high as her temper was to all other people, she never returned him a rough or impatient word. And she had a reward in the conviction of his deep, true affection for her, and in her aunt's entire and most sweet dependence upon her.

One day, however – it was near the end of November – Bessy had had a good deal to bear that seemed more than usually unreasonable on behalf of her uncle. The truth was that one of Kirkby's cows was ill, and John Kirkby was a good deal about in the farmyard; Bessy was interested about the animal, and had helped in preparing a mash over their own fire, that had to be given warm to the sick creature. If John had been out of the way, there would have been no one more anxious about the affair than Nathan, both because he was naturally kind-hearted and neighbourly, and also because he was rather proud of his reputation for knowledge in the diseases of cattle. But because John was about, and Bessy helping a little in what had to be done, Nathan would do nothing, and chose to assume that "nothing to think on ailed th' beast, but lads and lasses were allays fain to be feared on something". Now John was upwards of forty, and Bessy was nearly eight-and-twenty, so the terms lads and lasses did not exactly apply to their case.

When Bessy brought the milk in from their own cows towards half-past five o'clock, Nathan bade her make the doors, and not be running out i' the dark and cold about other folk's business, and, though Bessy was a little surprised and a good deal annoyed at his tone, she sat down to her supper without making a remonstrance. It had long been Nathan's custom to look out the last thing at night to see "what mak' o' weather it wur", and when towards half-past eight he got his stick and went out – two or three steps from the door which opened into the house place where they were sitting – Hester put her hand on her niece's shoulder and said:

"He's gotten a touch o' the rheumatics, as twinges him and makes him speak so sharp. I didna like to ask thee afore him, but how's yon poor beast?"

"Very ailing, belike. John Kirkby wur off for th' cow doctor when I cam in. I'll reckon they'll have to stop up wi't a'night."

Since their sorrows, her uncle had taken to reading a chapter in the Bible aloud, the last thing at night. He could not read fluently, and often hesitated long over a word, which he miscalled at length, but the very fact of opening the book seemed to soothe those old bereaved parents, for it made them feel quiet and safe in the presence of God, and took them out of the cares and troubles of this world into that futurity which, however dim and vague, was to their faithful hearts as a sure and certain rest. This little quiet time – Nathan sitting with his horn spectacles on; the tallow candle between him and his Bible, and throwing a strong light on his reverent, earnest face; Hester sitting on the other side of the fire, her head bowed in attentive listening, now and then shaking it, and moaning a little, but when a promise came, or any good tidings of great joy, saying "Amen" with fervour; Bessy by her aunt, perhaps her mind a little wandering to some household cares, or it might be on thoughts of those who were absent – this little quiet pause, I say, was grateful and soothing to this household, as a lullaby to a tired child. But this night, Bessy – sitting opposite to the long low window, only shaded by a few geraniums that grew in the sill, and the door alongside that window, through which her uncle had passed not a quarter of an hour before – saw the wooden latch of the door gently and almost noiselessly lifted up, as if someone were trying it from outside.

She was startled, and watched again intently, but it was perfectly still now. She thought it must have been that it had not fallen into its proper place when her uncle had come in and locked the door. It was just enough to make her uncomfortable, no more, and she almost persuaded herself it must have been fancy. Before she went upstairs, however, she went to the window to look out into the darkness, but all was still. Nothing to be seen; nothing to be heard. So the three went quietly upstairs to bed.

The house was little better than a cottage. The front door opened on a house place, over which was the old couple's bedroom. To the left, as you entered this pleasant house place and at close right angles with the entrance, was a door that led into the small parlour, which was Hester and Bessy's pride, although not half as comfortable as the house place, and never on any occasion used as a sitting room. There were shells and bunches of honesty in the fireplace; the best chest of drawers, and a company set of gaudy coloured china, and a bright common carpet on the floor, but all failed to give it the aspect of the homely comfort and delicate cleanliness of the house place. Over this parlour was the bedroom which Benjamin had slept in when a boy – when at home. It was kept still in a kind of readiness for him. The bed was still there, in which none had slept since he, eight or nine years ago, and every now and then the warming pan was taken quietly and silently up by his old mother, and the bed thoroughly aired. But this she did in her husband's absence, and without saying a word to anyone; nor did Bessy offer to help her, though her eyes often filled with tears, as she saw her aunt still going through the hopeless service. But the room had become a receptacle for unused things, and there was always a corner of it appropriated to the winter's store of apples. To the left of the house place, as you stood facing the fire, on the side opposite to the window and outer door, were two other doors; the one on the right opened into a kind of back kitchen, and had a lean-to roof, and a door opening onto the farmyard and back premises; the left hand door gave on the stairs, underneath which was a closet in which various household treasures were kept, and beyond that the dairy, over which Bessy slept; her little chamber window opening just above the sloping roof of the back kitchen. There were neither blinds nor shutters to any of the windows, either upstairs or down; the house was built of stone, and there was heavy framework of the same material round the little casement windows, and the long, low window of the house place was divided by what in grander dwellings would be called mullions.

By nine o'clock this night of which I am speaking, all had gone upstairs to bed; it was even later than usual, for the burning of candles was regarded so much in the light of extravagance, that the household kept early hours even for country folk. But somehow this evening, Bessy could not sleep, although in general she was in deep slumber five minutes after her head touched the pillow. Her thoughts ran on the chances for John Kirkby's cow, and a little fear lest the disorder might be epidemic, and spread to their own cattle. Across all these homely cares came a vivid, uncomfortable recollection of the way in which the door latch went up and down without any sufficient agency to account for it. She felt more sure now than she had done downstairs that it was a real movement and no effect of her imagination. She wished that it had not happened just when her uncle was reading, that she might at once have gone quick to the door, and convinced herself of the cause. As it was, her thoughts ran uneasily on the supernatural, and thence to Benjamin, her dear cousin and playfellow, her early lover. She had long given him up as lost for ever to her, if not actually dead, but this very giving him up for ever involved a free, full forgiveness of all his wrongs to her. She thought tenderly of him, as of one who might have been led astray in his later years, but who existed rather in her recollection as the innocent child, the spirited lad, the handsome, dashing young man. If John Kirkby's quiet attentions had ever betrayed his wishes to Bessy – if indeed he ever had any wishes on the subject – her first feeling would have been to compare his weather-beaten, middle-aged face and figure with the face and figure she remembered well, but never more expected to see in this life. So thinking, she became very restless, and weary of bed, and, after long tossing and turning, ending in a belief that she should never get to sleep at all that night, she went off soundly and suddenly.

As suddenly was she wide awake, sitting up in bed, listening to some noise that must have awakened her, but which was not repeated for some time. Surely it was in her uncle's room – her uncle was up, but for a minute or two there was no further sound. Then she heard him open his door, and go downstairs with hurried, tumbling steps. She now thought that her aunt must be ill, and hastily sprang out of bed, and was putting on her petticoat with hurried, trembling hands, and had just opened her chamber door, when she heard the front door undone, and a scuffle, as of the feet of several people, and many rude, passionate words, spoken hoarsely below the breath. Quick as thought she understood it all – the house was lonely – her uncle had the reputation of being well-to-do – they had pretended to be belated, and had asked their way or something. What a blessing that John Kirkby's cow was sick, for there were several men watching with him. She went back, opened her window, squeezed herself out, slid down the lean-to roof, and ran, barefoot and breathless, to the shippon.

"John, John, for the love of God come quick; there's robbers in the house, and Uncle and Aunt'll be murdered!" she whispered, in terrified accents, through the closed and barred shippon door. In a moment it was undone, and John and the cow doctor stood there, ready to act, if they but understood her rightly. Again she repeated her words, with broken, half-unintelligible explanations of what she as yet did not rightly understand.

"Front door is open, say's thou?" said John, arming himself with a pitchfork, while the cow doctor took some other implement. "Then I reckon we'd best make for that way o' getting into th' house, and catch 'em all in a trap."

"Run! Run!" was all Bessy could say, taking hold of John Kirkby's arm, and pulling him along with her. Swiftly did the three run to the house, round the corner, and in at the open front door. The men carried the horn lantern they had been using in the shippon, and, by the sudden oblong light that it threw upon objects, Bessy saw the principal one of her anxiety, her uncle, lying stunned and helpless on the kitchen floor. Her first thought was for him, for she had no idea that her aunt was in any immediate danger, although she heard the noise of feet, and fierce subdued voices upstairs.

"Make th' door behind us, lass. We'll not let them escape!" said brave John Kirkby, dauntless in a good cause, though he knew not how many there might be above. The cow doctor fastened and locked the door, saying, "There!" in a defiant tone, as he put the key in his pocket. It was to be a struggle for life or for death, or, at any rate, for effectual capture or desperate escape. Bessy kneeled down by her uncle, who did not speak nor give any sign of consciousness. Bessy raised his head by drawing a pillow off the settle and putting it under him; she longed to go for water into the back kitchen, but the sound of a violent struggle, and of heavy blows, and of low, hard curses spoken through closed teeth, and muttered passion, as though breath were too much needed for action to be wasted in speech, kept her still and quiet by her uncle's side in the kitchen, where the darkness might almost be felt, so thick and deep was it. Once – in a pause of her own heart's beating – a sudden terror came over her; she perceived, in that strange way in which the presence of a living creature forces itself on our consciousness in the darkest room, that someone was near her, keeping as still as she. It was not the poor old man's breathing that she heard, nor the radiation of his presence that she felt; someone else was in the kitchen; another robber, perhaps, left to guard the old man with murderous intent if his consciousness returned. Now, Bessy was fully aware that self-preservation would keep her terrible companion quiet, as there was no motive for his betraying himself stronger than the desire of escape – any effort for which he, the unseen witness, must know would be rendered abortive by the fact of the door being locked. Yet the knowledge that he was there, close to her, still, silent as the grave, with fearful, it might be deadly, unspoken thoughts in his heart, possibly even with keener and stronger sight than hers, as longer accustomed to the darkness, able to discern her figure and posture, and glaring at her like some wild beast, Bessy could not fail to shrink from the vision that her fancy presented. And still the struggle went on upstairs; feet slipping, blows sounding, and the wrench of intentioned aims, the strong gasps for breath, as the wrestlers paused for an instant. In one of these pauses Bessy felt conscious of a creeping movement close to her, which ceased when the noise of the strife above died away, and was resumed when it again began. She was aware of it by some subtle vibration of the air rather than by touch or sound. She was sure that he who had been close to her one minute as she knelt was, the next, passing stealthily towards the inner door which led to the staircase. She thought he was going to join and strengthen his accomplices, and, with a great cry, she sprang after him, but, just as she came to the doorway, through which some dim portion of light from the upper chambers came, she saw one man thrown downstairs with such violence that he fell almost at her very feet, while the dark, creeping figure glided suddenly away to the left, and as suddenly entered the closet beneath the stairs. Bessy had no time to wonder at his purpose in so doing, whether he had first designed to aid his accomplices in their desperate fight. He was an enemy, a robber, that was all she knew, and she sprang to the door of the closet, and in a trice had locked it on the outside. And then she stood frightened, panting in that dark corner, sick with terror lest the man who lay before her was either John Kirkby or the cow doctor. If it were either of those friendly two, what would become of the other – of her uncle, her aunt, herself? But in a very few minutes, this wonder was ended; her two defenders came slowly and heavily down the stairs, dragging with them a man, fierce, sullen, despairing – disabled with terrible blows, which had made his face one bloody, swollen mass. As for that, neither John nor the cow doctor were much more presentable. One of them bore the lantern in his teeth, for all their strength was taken up by the weight of the fellow they were bearing.

"Take care," said Bessy, from her corner, "there's a chap just beneath your feet. I dunno if he's dead or alive, and Uncle lies on the floor just beyond."

They stood still on the stairs for a moment. Just then the robber they had thrown downstairs stirred and moaned.

"Bessy," said John, "run off to th' stable and fetch ropes and gearing for to bind 'em, and we'll rid the house on 'em, and thou can'st go see after th' oud folks, who need it sadly."

Bessy was back in a very few minutes. When she came in, there was more light in the house place, for someone had stirred up the raked fire.

"That felly makes as though his legs were broken," said John, nodding towards the man still lying on the ground. Bessy felt almost sorry for him as they handled him – not over gently – and bound him, only half-conscious, as hardly and tightly as they had done his fierce, surly companion. She even felt so sorry for his evident agony, as they turned him over and over, that she ran to get him a cup of water to moisten his lips.

"I'm loth to leave yo' with him alone," said John, "though I'm thinking his leg is broken for sartain, and he can't stir, even if he comes to hissel, to do yo' any harm. But we'll just take off this chap, and make sure of him, and then one on us'll come back to yo' and we can, mebby, find a gate or so for ye to get shut on him out o' th' house. This felly's made safe enough, I'll be bound," said he, looking at the burglar, who stood, bloody and black, with fell hatred on his sullen face. His eye caught Bessy's as hers fell on him with dread so evident that it made him smile, and the look and the smile prevented the words from being spoken which were on Bessy's lips. She dared not tell, before him, that an able-bodied accomplice still remained in the house, lest somehow the door which kept him a prisoner should be broken open, and the fight renewed. So she only said to John, as he was leaving the house:

"Thou'lt not be long away, for I'm afeard of being left wi' this man."

"He'll noan do thee harm," said John.

"No! but I'm feared lest he should die. And there's Uncle and Aunt. Come back soon, John!"

"Ay, ay!" said he, half pleased. "I'll be back, never fear me."

So Bessy shut the door after them, but did not lock it for fear of mischances in the house, and went once more to her uncle, whose breathing, by this time, was easier than when she had first returned into the house place with John and the doctor. By the light of the fire, too, she could now see that he had received a blow on the head which was probably the occasion of his stupor. Round this wound, which was now bleeding pretty freely, Bessy put cloths dipped in cold water, and then, leaving him for a time, she lit a candle, and was about to go upstairs to her aunt, when, just as she was passing the bound and disabled robber, she heard her name softly, urgently called.

"Bessy, Bessy!" At first the voice sounded so close that she thought it must be the unconscious wretch at her feet. But once again that voice thrilled through her:

"Bessy, Bessy! For God's sake, let me out!"

She went to the stair-closet door, and tried to speak, but could not, her heart beat so terribly. Again, close to her ear:

"Bessy, Bessy! They'll be back directly; let me out, I say! For God's sake, let me out!" And he began to kick violently against the panels.

"Hush, hush!" she said, sick with a terrible dread, yet with a will strongly resisting her conviction. "Who are you?" But she knew – knew quite well.

"Benjamin." An oath. "Let me out, I say, and I'll be off, and out of England by tomorrow night never to come back, and you'll have all my father's money."

"D'ye think I care for that," said Bessy vehemently, feeling with trembling hands for the lock. "I wish there was noan such thing as money i' the world, afore yo'd come to this. There, yo're free, and I charge yo' never to let me see your face again. I'd ne'er ha let yo' loose but for fear of breaking their hearts, if yo' hanna killed them already." But before she had ended her speech, he was gone – off into the black darkness, leaving the door open wide. With a new terror in her mind, Bessy shut it afresh – shut it and bolted it this time. Then she sat down on the first chair, and relieved her soul by giving a great and exceeding bitter cry. But she knew it was no time for giving way, and, lifting herself up with as much effort as if each of her limbs was a heavy weight, she went into the back kitchen, and took a drink of cold water. To her surprise she heard her uncle's voice, saying feebly:

"Carry me up, and lay me by her."

But Bessy could not carry him; she could only help his faint exertions to walk upstairs, and, by the time he was there sitting panting on the first chair she could find, John Kirkby and Atkinson returned. John came up now to her aid. Her aunt lay across the bed in a fainting fit, and her uncle sat in so utterly broken-down a state that Bessy feared immediate death for both. But John cheered her up, and lifted the old man into his bed again, and, while Bessy tried to compose poor Hester's limbs into a position of rest, John went down to hunt about for the little store of gin which was always kept in a corner cupboard against emergencies.

"They've had a sore fright," said he, shaking his head, as he poured a little gin and hot water into their mouths with a teaspoon, while Bessy chafed their cold feet, "and it and the cold have been welly too much for 'em, poor old folk!"

He looked tenderly at them, and Bessy blessed him in her heart – blessed him unaware, for that look.

"I mun be off. I sent Atkinson up to th' farm for to bring down Bob, and Jack came wi' him back to th' shippon for to look after other man.

He began blackguarding us all round, so Bob and Jack were gagging wi' bridles when I left."

"Ne'er give heed to what he says," cried poor Bessy, a new panic besetting her. "Folks o' his sort are allays for dragging other folks into their mischief. I'm right glad he were well gagged."

"Well! but what I were saying were this. Atkinson and me will take t'other chap, who seems quiet enough, to th' shippon, and it'll be one piece o' work for to mind them and the cow, and I'll saddle old bay mare, and ride for constables and doctor fra Highminster. I'll bring Dr Preston up to see Nathan and Hester first, and then I reckon th' broken-legged chap down below must have his turn, for all he's met wi' his misfortunes in a wrong line o' life."

"Ay!" said Bessy. "We mun ha' the doctor sure enough, for look at them how they lie! Like two stone statues on a church monument, so sad and solemn."

"There's a look o' sense come back into their faces, though, sin' they supped that gin-and-water. I'd keep on a-bathing his head and giving them a sup on't fra time to time, if I was you, Bessy."

Bessy followed him downstairs, and lit the men out of the house. She dared not light them carrying their burden even, until they passed round the corner of the house, so strong was her fearful conviction that Benjamin was lurking near, seeking again to enter. She rushed back into the kitchen, bolted and barred the door, and pushed the end of the dresser against it, shutting her eyes as she passed the uncurtained window, for fear of catching a glimpse of a white face pressed against the glass, and gazing at her. The poor old couple lay quiet and speechless, although Hester's position had slightly altered: she had turned a little on her side towards her husband, and had laid one shrivelled arm around his neck. But he was just as Bessy had left him, with the wet clothes around his head, his eyes not wanting in a certain intelligence, but solemn, and unconscious to all that was passing around as the eyes of death.

His wife spoke a little from time to time – said a word of thanks, perhaps, or so: but he, never. All the rest of that terrible night Bessy tended the poor old couple with constant care, her own heart so stunned and bruised in its feelings that she went about her pious duties almost like one in a dream.

As far as Bessy could make out, the participation of that unnatural third was unknown; it was a relief, almost sickening in the revulsion it gave her from her terrible fear, which now she felt had haunted and held possession of her all night long, and had in fact paralysed her from thinking. Now she felt and thought with acute and feverish vividness, owing no doubt in part to the sleepless night she had passed. She felt almost sure that her uncle (possibly her aunt too) had recognized Benjamin, but there was a faint chance that they had not done so, and wild horses should never tear the secret from her, nor should any inadvertent word betray the fact that there had been a third person concerned. As to Nathan, he had never uttered a word. It was her aunt's silence that made Bessy fear lest Hester knew somehow that her son was concerned.

The doctor examined them both closely, looked hard at the wound on Nathan's head, asked questions which Hester answered shortly and unwillingly, and Nathan not at all, shutting his eyes as if even the sight of a stranger was pain to him. Bessy replied in their stead to all that she could answer respecting their state, and followed the doctor downstairs with a beating heart. When they came into the house place, they found John had opened the outer door to let in some fresh air, had brushed the hearth and made up the fire, and put the chairs and table in their right places. He reddened a little as Bessy's eye fell upon his swollen and battered face, but tried to smile it off in a dry kind of way.

"Yo' see I'm an ould bachelor, and I just thought as I'd redd up things a bit. How dun yo' find 'em, doctor?"

"Well, the poor old couple have had a terrible shock. I shall send them some soothing medicine to bring down the pulse, and a lotion for the old man's head. It is very well it bled so much; there might have been a good deal of inflammation." And so he went on, giving directions to Bessy for keeping them quietly in bed through the day. From these directions she gathered that they were not, as she had feared all night long, near to death. The doctor expected them to recover, though they would require care. She almost wished it had been otherwise, and that they, and she too, might have just lain down to their rest in the churchyard – so cruel did life seem to her; so dreadful the recollection of that subdued voice of the hidden robber, smiting her with recognition.

All this time John was getting things ready for breakfast, with something of the handiness of a woman. Bessy half-resented his officiousness in pressing Dr Preston to have a cup of tea, she did so want him to be gone and leave her alone with her thoughts. She did not know that all was done for love of her, that the hard-featured, short-spoken John was thinking all the time how ill and miserable she looked, and trying with tender artifices to make it incumbent upon her sense of hospitality to share Dr Preston's meal.

"I've seen as the cows is milked," said he, "yourn and all, and Atkinson's brought ours round fine. Whatten a marcy it were as she were sick just very night! Yon two chaps 'ud ha' made short work on't if yo' hadna fetched us in, and as it were we had a sore tussle. One on 'em'll bear the marks on't to his dying day, wunnot he, Doctor?"

"He'll barely have his leg well enough to stand his trial at York Assizes; they're coming off in a fortnight from now."

"Ay, and that reminds me, Bessy, yo'll have to go witness before Justice Royds. Constables bade me tell yo', and gie yo' this summons. Dunnot be feared; it will not be a long job, though I'm not saying as it'll be a pleasant one. Yo'll have to answer questions as to how, and all about it, and Jane" (his sister) "will come and stop wi' th' oud folks, and I'll drive yo' in the shandry."

No one knew why Bessy's colour blanched, and her eye clouded. No one knew how she apprehended lest she should have to say that Benjamin had been of the gang, if, indeed, in some way the law had not followed on his heels quick enough to catch him.

But that trial was spared her; she was warned by John to answer questions, and say no more than was necessary, for fear of making her story less clear, and as she was known, by character, at least to Justice Royds and his clerk, they made the examination as little formidable as possible.

When all was over, and John was driving her back again, he expressed his rejoicing that there would be evidence enough to convict the men without summoning Nathan and Hester to identify them. Bessy was so tired that she hardly understood what an escape it was – how far greater than even her companion understood.

Jane Kirkby stayed with her for a week or more, and was an unspeakable comfort. Otherwise she sometimes thought she should have gone mad, with the face of her uncle always reminding her, in its stony expression of agony, of that fearful night. Her aunt was softer in her sorrow, as became one of her faithful and pious nature, but it was easy to see how her heart bled inwardly. She recovered her strength sooner than her husband, but as she recovered, the doctor perceived the rapid approach of total blindness. Every day, nay, every hour of the day, that Bessy dared, without fear of exciting their suspicions of her knowledge, she told them, as she had anxiously told them at first, that only two men, and those perfect strangers, had been discovered as being concerned in the burglary. Her uncle would never have asked a question about it, even if she had withheld all information about the affair, but she noticed the quick, watching, waiting glance of his eye whenever she returned from any person or place where she might have been supposed to gain intelligence if Benjamin were suspected or caught, and she hastened to relieve the old man's anxiety by always telling all that she had heard, thankful that as the days passed on the danger she sickened to think of grew less and less.

Day by day Bessy had ground for thinking that Aunt knew more than she had apprehended at first. There was something so very humble and touching in Hester's blind way of feeling about for her husband – stern, woe-begone Nathan – and mutely striving to console him in the deep agony of which Bessy learnt from this loving, piteous manner that her aunt was conscious. Her aunt's face looked blankly up into his, tears slowly running down from her sightless eyes, while from time to time, when she thought herself unheard by any save him, she would repeat such texts as she had heard at church in happier days, and which she thought, in her true, simple piety, might tend to console him. Yet day by day her aunt grew more and more sad.

Three or four days before assize time, two summonses to attend the trial at York were sent to the old people. Neither Bessy, nor John, nor Jane, could understand this, for their own notices had come long before, and they had been told that their evidence would be enough to convict.

But alas! the fact was that the lawyer employed to defend the prisoners had heard from them that there was a third person engaged, and had heard who that third person was, and it was this advocate's business to diminish if possible the guilt of his clients by proving that they were but tools in the hands of one who had, from his superior knowledge of the premises and the daily customs of the inhabitants, been the originator and planner of the whole affair. To do this it was necessary to have the evidence of the parents, who, as the prisoners had said, must have recognized the voice of the young man, their son. For no one knew that Bessy, too, could have borne witness to his having been present, and, as it was supposed that Benjamin had escaped out of England, there was no exact betrayal of him on the part of his accomplices.

Wondering, bewildered and weary, the old couple reached York, in company with John and Bessy, on the eve of the day of trial. Nathan was still so self-contained that Bessy could never guess what had been passing in his mind. He was almost passive under his old wife's trembling caresses; he seemed hardly conscious of them, so rigid was his demeanour.

She, Bessy feared at times, was becoming childish, for she had evidently so great and anxious a love for her husband that her memory seemed going in her endeavours to melt the stoniness of his aspect and manners; she appeared occasionally to have forgotten why he was so changed, in her piteous little attempts to bring him back to his former self.

"They'll for sure never torture them when they see what old folks they are!" cried Bessy, on the morning of the trial, a dim fear looming over her mind. "They'll never be so cruel, for sure!"

But "for sure" it was so. The barrister looked up at the judge almost apologetically, as he saw how hoary-headed and woeful an old man was put into the witness box when the defence came on, and Nathan Huntroyd was called on for his evidence.

"It is necessary, on behalf of my clients, my lord, that I should pursue a course which, for all other reasons, I deplore."

"Go on!" said the judge. "What is right and legal must be done." But, an old man himself, he covered his quivering mouth with his hand as Nathan, with grey, unmoved face, and solemn, hollow eyes, placing his two hands on each side of the witness box, prepared to give his answers to questions, the nature of which he was beginning to foresee, but would not shrink from replying to truthfully; "the very stones" (as he said to himself, with a kind of dulled sense of the Eternal Justice) "rise up against such a sinner."

"Your name is Nathan Huntroyd, I believe?"

"It is."

"You live at Nab End Farm?"

"I do."

"Do you remember the night of November the twelfth?"

"Yes."

"You were awakened that night by some noise, I believe. What was it?"

The old man's eyes fixed themselves upon his questioner with a look of a creature brought to bay. That look the barrister never forgets. It will haunt him till his dying day.

"It was a throwing up of stones against our window."

"Did you hear it at first?"

"No."

"What awakened you, then?"

"She did."

"And then you both heard the stones. Did you hear nothing else?"

A long pause. Then a low, clear, "Yes."

"What?"

"Our Benjamin asking us for to let him in. She said as it were him, leastways."

"And you thought it was him, did you not?"

"I told her" (this time in a louder voice) "for to get to sleep, and not to be thinking every drunken chap as passed by were our Benjamin, for that he were dead and gone."

"And she?"

"She said as though she'd heerd our Benjamin afore she were welly awake, axing for to be let in. But I bade her ne'er heed her dreams, but turn on her other side, and get to sleep again."

"And did she?"

A long pause – judge, jury, bar, audience, all held their breath. At length Nathan said:

"No!"

"What did you do then? (My lord I am compelled to ask these painful questions.)"

"I saw she wadna be quiet; she had allays thought he would come back to us, like the Prodigal i' the Gospels." (His voice choked a little, but he tried to make it steady, succeeded, and went on.) "She said if I wadna get up she would, and just then I heerd a voice. I'm not quite mysel, gentlemen – I've been ill and i' bed, an' it makes me trembling-like. Someone said, 'Father, Mother, I'm here, starving i' the cold – wunnot yo' get up and let me in?'"

"And that voice was?"

"It were like our Benjamin's. I see whatten yo're driving at, sir, and I'll tell yo' truth, though it kills me to speak it. I dunnot say it were our Benjamin as spoke, mind yo' – I only say it were like—"

"That's all I wanted, my good fellow. And on the strength of that entreaty, spoken in your son's voice, you went down and opened the door to these two prisoners at the bar, and to a third man?"

Nathan nodded assent, and even that counsel was too merciful to force him to put more into words.

"Call Hester Huntroyd."

An old woman, with a face of which the eyes were evidently blind, with a sweet, gentle, careworn face, came into the witness box, and meekly curtsyed to the presence of those whom she had been taught to respect – a presence she could not see.

There was something in her humble, blind aspect, as she stood waiting to have something done to her – what, her poor troubled mind hardly knew – that touched all who saw her inexpressibly. Again the counsel apologized, but the judge could not reply in words; his face was quivering all over, and the jury looked uneasily at the prisoners' counsel. That gentleman saw that he might go too far, and send their sympathies off on the other side, but one or two questions he must ask. So, hastily recapitulating much that he had learnt from Nathan, he said, "You believed it was your son's voice asking to be let in?"

"Ay! Our Benjamin came home, I'm sure; choose where he is gone."

She turned her head about, as if listening for the voice of her child, in the hushed silence of the court.

"Yes; he came home that night – and your husband went down to let him in?"

"Well! I believe he did. There was a great noise of folk down stair."

"And you heard your son Benjamin's voice among the others?"

"Is it to do him harm, sir?" asked she, her face growing more intelligent and intent on the business in hand.

"That is not my object in questioning you. I believe he has left England, so nothing you can say will do him any harm. You heard your son's voice, I say?"

"Yes, sir. For sure, I did."

"And some men came upstairs into your room? What did they say?"

"They axed where Nathan kept his stocking."

"And you – did you tell them?"

"No, sir, for I knew Nathan would not like me to."

"What did you do then?"

A shade of reluctance came over her face, as if she began to perceive causes and consequences.

"I just screamed on Bessy – that's my niece, sir."

"And you heard someone shout out from the bottom of the stairs?"

She looked piteously at him, but did not answer.

"Gentlemen of the jury, I wish to call your particular attention to this fact: she acknowledges she heard someone shout – some third person, you observe – shout out to the two above. What did he say? That is the last question I shall trouble you with. What did the third person, left behind downstairs, say?"

Her face worked – her mouth opened two or three times as if to speak – she stretched out her arms imploringly, but no word came, and she fell back into the arms of those nearest to her. Nathan forced himself forwards into the witness box:

"My Lord Judge, a woman bore ye, as I reckon; it's a cruel shame to serve a mother so. It wur my son, my only child, as called out for us t'open door, and who shouted out for to hold th' oud woman's throat if she did na stop her noise, when hoo'd fain ha' cried for her niece to help. And now yo've the truth, and a' th' truth, and I'll leave you to th' Judgment o' God for th' way yo've getten at it."

Before night the mother was stricken with paralysis, and lay on her deathbed. But the broken-hearted go home, to be comforted of God.

8

The Ghost in the Corner Room

by Charles Dickens

I HAD OBSERVED Mr Governor growing fidgety as his turn – his "spell", he called it – approached, and he now surprised us all by rising with a serious countenance, and requesting permission to "come aft" and have speech with me, before he spun his yarn. His great popularity led to a gracious concession of this indulgence, and we went out together into the hall.

"Old shipmate," said Mr Governor to me, "ever since I have been aboard this old hulk, I have been haunted, day and night."

"By what, Jack?"

Mr Governor, clapping his hand on my shoulder and keeping it there, said:

"By something of the likeness of a woman."

"Ah! Your old affliction. You'll never get over *that*, Jack, if you live to be a hundred."

"No, don't talk so, because I am very serious. All night long, I have been haunted by one figure. All day, the same figure has so bewildered me in the kitchen, that I wonder I haven't poisoned the whole ship's company. Now, there's no fancy here. Would you like to see the figure?"

"I should like to see it very much."

"Then here it is!" said Jack. Thereupon, he presented my sister, who had stolen out quietly, after us.

"Oh, indeed?" said I. "Then, I suppose, Patty, my dear, I have no occasion to ask whether *you* have been haunted?"

"Constantly, Joe," she replied.

The effect of our going back again, all three together, and of my presenting my sister as the Ghost from the Corner Room, and Jack as the Ghost from my Sister's Room, was triumphant – the crowning hit of the night. Mr Beaver was so particularly delighted that he by and by declared a very little would make him dance a hornpipe. Mr Governor immediately supplied the very little by offering to make it a double hornpipe, and there ensued such toe-and-heeling, and buckle-covering, and double-shuffling, and heel-sliding, and execution of all sorts of slippery manoeuvres with vibratory legs, as none of us ever saw before, or will ever see again. When we had all laughed and applauded till we were faint, Starling, not to be outdone, favoured us with a more modern saltatory entertainment in the Lancashire clog manner – to the best of my belief, the longest dance ever performed – in which the sound of his feet became a locomotive going through cuttings, tunnels and open country, and became a vast number of other things we should never have suspected, unless he had kindly told us what they were.

It was resolved before we separated that night that our three months' period in the Haunted House should be wound up with the marriage of my sister and Mr Governor. Belinda was nominated bridesmaid, and Starling was engaged for bridegroom's man.

In a word, we lived our term out most happily, and were never for a moment haunted by anything more disagreeable than our own imaginations and remembrances. My cousin's wife, in her great love for her husband and in her gratitude to him for the change her love had wrought in her, had told us, through his lips, her own story, and I am sure there was not one of us who did not like her the better for it, and respect her the more.

So, at last, before the shortest month in the year was quite out, we all walked forth one morning to the church with the spire, as if nothing uncommon were going to happen, and there Jack and my sister were married, as sensibly as could be. It occurs to me that I observed Belinda and Alfred Starling to be rather sentimental and low, on the occasion, and they are since engaged to be married in the same church. I regard it as an excellent thing for both, and a kind of union very wholesome for the times in which we live. He wants a little poetry, and she wants a little prose, and the marriage of the two things is the happiest marriage I know for all mankind.

Finally, I derived this Christmas greeting from the Haunted House, which I affectionately address with all my heart to all my readers: – Let us use the great virtue, Faith, but not abuse it, and let us put it to its best use, by having faith in the great Christmas book of the New Testament, and in one another.

Note on the Text

The text in the present edition is based on the first printing in *All the Year Round* in 1862. The spelling and punctuation have been standardized, modernized and made consistent throughout.

Notes

p. 11, *the Admirable Crichton*: A reference to James Crichton (1560–82), the Scottish polymath and man of letters.

p. 12, *Rhadamanthus*: A legendary king in Greek mythology, the son of Zeus and one of the judges of the dead.

p. 22, *Magnall's Questions*: *Historical and Miscellaneous Questions for the Use of Young People* (1800), by Richmal Magnall (1769–1820), was a standard reference work in the nineteenth century.

Extra Material

on

Charles Dickens's

The Haunted House

Charles Dickens's Life

Charles John Huffam Dickens was born in Portsmouth on 7th February 1812 to John Dickens and Elizabeth Dickens, née Barrow. His father worked as a navy payroll clerk at the local dockyard, before transferring and moving his family to London in 1814, and then to Kent in 1817. It seems that this period possessed an idyllic atmosphere for ever afterwards in Dickens's mind. Much of his childhood was spent reading and rereading the books in his father's library, which included *Robinson Crusoe*, *The Vicar of Wakefield*, *Don Quixote*, Fielding, Smollett and the *Arabian Nights*. He was a promising, prize-winning pupil at school, and generally distinguished by his cleverness, sensitivity and enthusiasm, although unfortunately this was tempered by his frail and sickly constitution. It was at this time that he also had his first experience of what would become one of the abiding passions in his life: the theatre. Sadly, John Dickens's finances had become increasingly unhealthy, a situation which was worsened when he was transferred to London in 1822. This relocation, which entailed a termination in his schooling, distressed Charles, though he slowly came to be fascinated with the teeming, squalid streets of London.

In London, however, family finances continued to plummet until the Dickenses were facing bankruptcy. A family connection, James Lamert, offered to employ Charles at the Warren's Blacking Warehouse, which he was managing, and Dickens started working there in February 1824. He spent between six months and a year there, and the experience would prove to have a profound and lasting effect on him. The work was drudgery – sealing and labelling pots of black paste all day – and his only companions were uneducated working-class boys. His discontent at the situation was compounded by the fact that his talented older sister was sent to the Royal Academy of Music, while he was left in the warehouse.

John Dickens was finally arrested for debt and taken to Marshalsea Prison in Southwark on 20th February 1824, his wife and children (excluding Charles) moving in with him in order to save money. Meanwhile, Charles found lodgings with an intimidating old lady called Mrs Roylance (on whom he apparently modelled Mrs Pipchin in *Dombey and Son*) in Little College Street, later moving to Lant Street in Borough, which was closer to the prison. At the end of May 1824, John Dickens was released, and gradually paid off creditors as he attempted to start a new life for himself and his family. However, for some time afterwards Charles reluctantly pursued his employment at the blacking factory, as it seems his mother was unwilling to take him out of it, and even tried to arrange for him to return after he did leave. It appears that he was only removed from the warehouse after his father had quarrelled with James Lamert. The stint at the blacking factory was so profoundly humiliating for Dickens that throughout his life he apparently never mentioned this experience to any of those close to him, revealing it only in a fragment of a memoir written in 1848 and presented to his biographer John Forster: "No words can express the secret agony of my soul as I sunk into this companionship, compared these everyday associates with those of my happier childhood, and felt my early hopes of growing up to be a learned and distinguished man crushed in my breast."

School and Work in London

Fortunately he was granted some respite from hard labour when he was sent to be educated at the Wellington House Academy on Hampstead Road. Although the standard of teaching he received was apparently mediocre, the two years he spent at the school were idyllic compared to his warehouse experience, and Charles took advantage of them by making friends his own age and participating in school drama. Regrettably he had to leave the Academy in 1827, when the family finances were in turmoil once again. He found employment as a junior clerk in a solicitor's office, a job that, although routine and somewhat unfulfilling, enabled Dickens to become familiar with the ways of the London courts and the jargon of the legal profession – which he would later frequently lampoon in his novels. On reaching his eighteenth birthday, Dickens enrolled as a reader at the British Museum, determined to make up for the inadequacies of his education by studying the books in its collection, and taught himself shorthand in the hope of taking on journalistic work.

In less than a year he set himself up as a freelance law reporter, initially covering the civil law courts known as Doctors' Commons – which he did with some brio, though he found it slightly tedious – and in 1831 advanced to the press gallery of the House of Commons. His reputation as a reporter was growing steadily, and in 1834 he joined the staff of the *Morning Chronicle*, one of the leading daily newspapers. During this period, he observed and commented on some of the most socially significant debates of the time, such as the Reform Act of 1832, the Factory Act of 1833 and the Poor Law Amendment Act of 1834.

In 1829, he fell in love with the flirtatious and beautiful Maria *First Love* Beadnell, the daughter of a wealthy banker, and he seems to have remained fixated on her for several years, although she rebuffed his advances. This disappointment spurred him on to achieve a higher station in life, and – after briefly entertaining the notion of becoming an actor – he threw himself into his work and wrote short stories in his spare time, which he had published in magazines, although without pay.

Soon enough his work for the *Morning Chronicle* was not *Marriage and First* limited to covering parliamentary matters: in recognition of *Major Publication* his capacity for descriptive writing, he was encouraged to write reviews and sketches, and cover important meetings, dinners and election campaigns – which he reported on with enthusiasm. Written under the pseudonym "Boz", his sketches on London street life – published in the *Morning Chronicle* and then also in its sister paper, the *Evening Chronicle* – were highly rated and gained a popular following. Things were also looking up in Dickens's personal life, as he fell in love with Catherine Hogarth, the daughter of the editor of the *Evening Chronicle*: they became engaged in May 1835, and married on 2nd April 1836 at St Luke's Church in Chelsea, honeymooning in Kent afterwards. At this time his literary career began to gain momentum: first his writings on London were compiled under the title *Sketches by Boz* and printed in an illustrated two-volume edition, and then, just a few days before his wedding, *The Pickwick Papers* began to be published in monthly instalments – becoming the best-selling serialization since Lord Byron's *Childe Harold's Pilgrimage*.

At the end of 1836, Dickens resigned from the *Morning* *Success* *Chronicle* to concentrate on his literary endeavours, and met

John Forster, who was to remain a lifelong friend. He helped Dickens to manage the business and legal side of his life, as well as acting as a trusted literary adviser and biographer. Forster's acumen for resolving complex situations was particularly welcome at this point, since, following the resounding success of *The Pickwick Papers*, Dickens had over-committed himself to a number of projects, with newspapers and publishers eager to capitalize on the latest literary sensation, and the deals and payments agreed no longer reflected his stature as an author.

In January 1837, Catherine gave birth to the couple's first child, also called Charles, which prompted the young Dickens family to move from their lodgings in Furnival's Inn in Holborn to a house on 48 Doughty Street. The following month *Oliver Twist* started appearing in serial form in *Bentley's Miscellany*, which lifted the author's name to new heights. This period of domestic bliss and professional fulfilment was tragically interrupted when Catherine's sister Mary suddenly died in May at the age of seventeen. Dickens was devastated and had to interrupt work on *The Pickwick Papers* and *Oliver Twist*; this event would have a deep impact on his world view and his art. But his literary productivity would soon continue unabated; hot on the tail of *Oliver Twist* came *Nicholas Nickleby* (1838–39) and *The Old Curiosity Shop* (1840–41). By this stage, he was the leading author of the day, frequenting high society and meeting luminaries such as his idol, Thomas Carlyle. Consequently he moved to a grand Georgian house near Regent's Park, and frequently holidayed in a house in Broadstairs in Kent.

Whereas his previous novels had all more or less followed his successful formula of comedy, melodrama and social satire, Dickens opted for a different approach for his next major work, *Barnaby Rudge*, a purely historical novel. He found the writing of this book particularly arduous, so he decided that after five years of intensive labour he needed a sabbatical, and persuaded his publishers Chapman and Hall to grant him a year's leave with a monthly advance of £150 on his future earnings. During this year he would visit America and keep a notebook on his travels, with a view to getting it published on his return.

First Visit to America   Dickens journeyed by steamship to Halifax, Nova Scotia, accompanied by his wife, in January 1842, and the couple would spend almost five months travelling around North America, visiting cities such as Boston, New York, Philadelphia, Cincinnati, Louisville, Toronto and Montreal. He was greeted by crowds of enthusiastic well-wishers wherever he went, and met countless important figures such as Henry Wadsworth Longfellow, Edgar Allan Poe and President John Tyler, but after the initial exhilaration of this fanfare he found it exhausting and overwhelming. The trip also brought about its share of disillusionment: having cherished romantic dreams of America being free from the corruption and snobbery of Europe, he was increasingly appalled by certain aspects of the New World, such as slavery, the treatment of prisoners and, perhaps most of all, the refusal of America to sign an international copyright agreement to prevent his works being pirated in America. He wrote articles and made speeches condemning these practices, which resulted in a considerable amount of press hostility.

Having returned to England in the summer of 1842, he *Back Home*
published his record of the trip under the title of *American Notes* and the first instalment of *Martin Chuzzlewit* later that year. Unfortunately neither of the two were quite as successful as he or his publishers would have hoped, although Dickens believed *Martin Chuzzlewit* (1842–44) was his finest work to date. During this period, Dickens started taking a greater interest in political and social issues, particularly in the treatment of children employed in mines and factories, and in the "ragged school" movement, which provided free education for destitute children. He became acquainted with the millionaire philanthropist Angela Burdett-Coutts, and persuaded her to give financial support to a school in London. In 1843, he decided to write a seasonal tale which would highlight the plight of the poor, publishing *A Christmas Carol* to great popular success in December 1843. The following year Dickens decided to leave Chapman and Hall, as his relations with them had become increasingly strained, and persuaded his printer Bradbury and Evans to become his new publisher.

In July 1844 Dickens relocated his entire family to *Move to Genoa*
Genoa in order to escape London and find new sources of inspiration – and also because life in Italy was considerably cheaper. Dickens, although at first taken aback by the decay of the Ligurian capital, appears to have been fascinated by this new country and a quick learner of its language and customs. He did not write much there, apart from another Christmas book, *The Chimes*, the publication of which occasioned a brief return to London. In all the Dickenses remained in Italy for a year, travelling around the country

for three months in early 1845, before returning to England in July of that year.

In Italy, he discovered that he was apparently able mesmerically to alleviate the condition of Augusta de la Rue, the wife of a Swiss banker, who suffered from anxiety and nervous spasms. This treatment required him to spend a lot of time alone with her, and unsurprisingly Catherine was not best pleased by this turn of events. She was also worn out by the burden of motherhood: they were becoming a large family, and would eventually have a total of ten children. Catherine's sister Georgina therefore began to help out with the children. Georgina was in many ways similar to Mary, whose death had so devastated Dickens, and she became involved with Dickens's various projects.

Back in London, Dickens took part in amateur theatrical productions, and took on the task of editing the *Daily News*, a new national newspaper owned by Bradbury and Evans. However, he had severely underestimated the work involved in editing the publication and resigned after seventeen issues, though he did continue to write contributions, including a series of 'Travelling Letters' – later collected in *Pictures from Italy* (1846).

More Travels Abroad   Perhaps to escape the aftermath of his resignation from the *Daily News* and to focus on composing his next novel, Dickens moved his family to Lausanne in Switzerland. He enjoyed the clean, quiet and beautiful surroundings, as well as the company of the town's fellow English expatriates. He also managed to write fiction: another Christmas tale entitled *The Battle of Life* and, more significantly, the beginning of *Dombey and Son*, which began serialization in September 1846 and was an immediate success.

It was also at this point that his publisher launched a series of cheap editions of his works, in the hope of tapping into new markets. Dickens returned to London, and resumed his normal routine of socializing, amateur theatricals, letter-writing and public speaking, and also became deeply involved in charitable work, such as setting up and administering a shelter for homeless women, which was funded by Miss Burdett-Coutts. *The Haunted Man*, another Christmas story, appeared in 1848, and was followed by his next major novel, *David Copperfield* (1849–50), which received rapturous critical acclaim.

Household Words   *Household Words* was set up at this time, a popular magazine founded and edited by Dickens himself. The magazine contained fictional work by not only Dickens, but also contributors such as Gaskell and Wilkie Collins, and articles on social issues. Dickens continued with his amateur theatricals, which proved a welcome distraction, since Catherine was quite seriously ill, as was his father, who died shortly afterwards. This was followed by the sudden death of his eight-month-old daughter Dora.

The Dickenses moved house again in November 1851, this time to Tavistock House in Tavistock Square. Since it was in a dilapidated state, renovation was necessary, and Dickens personally supervised every detail of this, from the installation of new plumbing to the choice of wallpaper. *Bleak House* (1852–53), his next publication, sold well, though straight after finishing it, Dickens was in desperate need of a break. He went on holiday in France with his family, and then toured Italy with Wilkie Collins and the painter Augustus Egg. After his return to London, Dickens gave a series of public readings to larger audiences than he had been accustomed to. Dickens's histrionic talents thrived in this context and the readings were a triumph, encouraging the author to repeat the exercise throughout his career – indeed, this became a lucrative venture, with Dickens employing his friend Arthur Smith as his booking agent.

During this period Dickens's stance on current politics and society became increasingly critical, which manifested itself in the numerous satirical essays he penned and the darker, more trenchant outlook of *Bleak House* and the two novels that followed, *Hard Times* (1854) and *Little Dorrit* (1855–57). In March 1856, Dickens bought Gad's Hill Place, near Rochester, for use as a country home. He had admired it during childhood country walks with his father, who had told him he might eventually own it if he were very hard-working and persevering.

However, this acquisition of a permanent home was not accompanied by domestic felicity, as by this point Dickens's marriage was in crisis. Relations between Dickens and his wife had been worsening for some time, but it all came to a head when he became acquainted with a young actress by the name of Ellen Ternan and apparently fell in love with her. The affair may never have been consummated, but Dickens involved himself with Ellen and her family's life to an extent which alarmed Catherine, just as she had been alarmed by the excessive attentions he had paid to Mme de la Rue in Genoa. Soon enough, Dickens moved into a

The End of the Marriage

separate bedroom in their house, and in May 1858, Dickens and his wife formally separated. This gave rise to a flurry of speculation, including rumours that Dickens was involved in a relationship with the young actress, or even worse, his sister-in-law, Georgina Hogarth, who had opted to continue living with Dickens instead of with her sister. It seemed that some of these allegations may have originated from the Hogarths, his wife's immediate family, and Dickens reacted to this by forcing them to sign a retraction, and by issuing a public statement – against his friends' advice – in *The Times* and *Household Words*. Furthermore, in August of that year one of Dickens's private letters was leaked to the press, which placed the blame for the breakdown of their marriage entirely on Catherine's shoulders, accused her of being a bad mother and insinuated that she was mentally unstable. After some initial protests, Catherine made no further effort to defend herself, and lived a quiet life until her death twenty years later. She apparently never met Dickens again, but never stopped caring about him, and followed his career and publications assiduously.

All the Year Round   This conflict in Dickens's personal affairs also had an effect on his professional life: in 1859 the author fell out with Bradbury and Evans after they had refused to run another statement about his private life in one of their publications, the satirical magazine *Punch*. This led him to transfer back to Chapman and Hall and to found a new weekly periodical *All the Year Round*. His first contribution to the magazine was his highly successful second historical novel, *A Tale of Two Cities* (1859), an un-Dickensian work in that it was more or less devoid of comical and satirical elements. *All the Year Round* – which focused more on fiction and less on journalistic pieces than its predecessor – maintained very healthy circulation figures, especially as the second novel to be serialized was the tremendously popular *The Woman in White* by Wilkie Collins, who became a regular collaborator. Dickens also arranged with the New York publisher J.M. Emerson & Co. for his journal to appear across the Atlantic. In December 1860, Dickens began to serialize what would become one of his best-loved novels, the deeply autobiographical *Great Expectations* (1860–61).

Our Mutual   Between the final instalment of *Great Expectations* and *Friend* the first instalment of his next and final completed novel, *Our Mutual Friend*, there was an uncharacteristically long three-year gap. This period was marked by two deaths in the family in 1863: that of his mother – which came as a relief more than anything, as she had been declining into senility for some time, and Dickens's feeling for her were ambivalent at best – and that of his second son, Walter – for whom Dickens grieved much more deeply. He chewed over ideas for *Our Mutual Friend* for at least two years and only began seriously composing it in early 1864, with serialization beginning in May. Although the book is now widely considered a masterpiece, it met with a tepid reception at the time, as readers did not entirely understand it.

On 9th June 1865, Dickens experienced a traumatic incident: travelling back from France with Ellen Ternan and her mother, he was involved in a serious railway accident at Staplehurst, in which ten people lost their lives. Dickens was physically unharmed, but nevertheless profoundly affected by it, having spent hours tending the dying and injured with brandy. He drew on the experience in the writing of one of his best short stories, 'The Signalman'. *Staplehurst Train Disaster*

Following the success of his public readings in Britain, Dickens had been contemplating a tour of the United States, and finally embarked on a second trip to America from December 1867 to April 1868. This turned out to be a very lucrative visit, but the exhaustion occasioned by his punishing schedule proved to be disastrous for his health. He began a farewell tour around England in 1868, incorporating a spectacular piece derived from *Oliver Twist*'s scene of Nancy's murder, but was forced to abandon the tour on the instructions of his doctors after he had a stroke in April 1869. Against medical advice, he insisted on giving a series of twelve final readings in London in 1870. These were very well received, many of those who attended commenting that he had never read so well as then. While in London, he had a private audience with Queen Victoria, and met the Prime Minister. *Final Years*

Dickens immersed himself in writing another major novel, *The Mystery of Edwin Drood*, the first six instalments of which were a critical and financial success. Tragically this novel was never to be completed, as Dickens died on 9th June 1870, having suffered a stroke on the previous day. He had wished to be buried in a small graveyard in Rochester, but this was overridden by a nationwide demand that he should be laid to rest in Westminster Abbey. This was done on 14th June 1870, after a strictly private ceremony which he had insisted on in his will. *Death*

Charles Dickens's Works

As seen in the account of his life above, Charles Dickens was an immensely prolific writer, not only of novels but of countless articles, sketches, occasional writings and travel accounts, published in newspapers, magazines and in volume form. Descriptions of his most famous works can be found below.

Sketches by Boz   *Sketches by Boz*, a revised and expanded collection of Dickens's newspaper pieces, was published in two volumes by John Macrone on 8th February 1836. The book was composed of sketches of London life, manners and society. It was an immediate success, and was praised by critics for the "startling fidelity" of its descriptions.

The Pickwick Papers   The first instalment of Dickens's first serialized novel, *The Pickwick Papers*, appeared in March 1836. Initially Dickens's contributions were subordinate to those of the illustrator Robert Seymour, but as the series continued, this relationship was inverted, with Dickens's writing at the helm. This led to an upsurge in sales, until *The Pickwick Papers* became a fully fledged literary phenomenon, with circulation rocketing to 40,000 by the final instalment in November 1837. The book centres around the Pickwick Club and its founder, Mr Pickwick, who travels around the country with his companions Mr Winkle, Mr Snodgrass and Mr Tupman, and consists of various loosely connected and light-hearted adventures, with hints of the social satire which would pervade his mature fiction. There is no overall plot, as Dickens invented one episode at a time and, reacting to popular feedback, would switch the emphasis to the most successful characters.

Oliver Twist   Dickens's first coherently structured novel, *Oliver Twist*, was serialized in *Bentley's Miscellany* from February 1837 to April 1839, with illustrations by the famous caricaturist George Cruikshank. Subtitled *A Parish Boy's Progress*, in reference to Hogarth's *A Rake's Progress* and *A Harlot's Progress* cycles, Dickens tells the story of a young orphan's life and ordeals in London – which had never before been the substance of a novel – as he flees the workhouse and unhappy apprenticeship of his childhood to London, where he falls in with a criminal gang led by the malicious Fagin, before eventually discovering the secret of his origins. *Oliver Twist* publicly addressed issues such as workhouses and child exploitation by criminals – and this preoccupation with social ills and the plight of the downtrodden would become a hallmark of Dickens's fiction.

Dickens's next published novel – the serialization of which *Nicholas Nickleby* for a while overlapped with that of *Oliver Twist* – was *Nicholas Nickleby*, which revolves around its eponymous hero – again an impoverished young man, though an older one this time – as he tenaciously overcomes the odds to establish himself in the world. When Nicholas's father dies penniless, the family turn to their uncle Ralph Nickleby for assistance, but he turns out to be a mean-spirited miser, and only secures menial positions for Nicholas and his sister Kate. Nicholas is sent to work in Dotheboys Hall, a dreadful Yorkshire boarding school administered by the schoolmaster Wackford Squeers, while Kate endures a humiliating stint at a London millinery. The plot twists and turns until both end up finding love and a secure position in life. Dickens's satire is more trenchant, particularly with regard to Yorkshire boarding schools, which were notorious at the time. Interestingly, within ten years of *Nicholas Nickleby*'s publication all the schools in question were closed down. Overall though, the tone is jovial and the plot is rambling and entertaining, much in the vein of Dickens's eighteenth-century idols Fielding and Smollett.

The Old Curiosity Shop started out as a piece in the short- *The Old Curiosity Shop* lived weekly magazine that Dickens was editing, *Master Humphrey's Clock*, which began publication in April 1840. It was intended to be a miscellany of one-off stories, but as sales were disappointing, Dickens was forced to adapt the 'Personal Adventures of Master Humphrey' into a full-length narrative that would be the most Romantic and fairy-tale-like of Dickens's novels, with some of his greatest humorous passages. The story revolves around Little Nell, a young girl who lives with her grandfather in his eponymous shop, and recounts how the two struggle to release themselves from the grip of the evil usurer dwarf Quilp. By the end of its serialization, circulation had reached the phenomenal figure of 100,000, and Little Nell's death had famously plunged thousands of readers into grief.

As seen above, Dickens took on a different genre for his *Barnaby Rudge* next major work of fiction, *Barnaby Rudge*: this was a historical novel, addressing the anti-Catholic Gordon riots of 1780, which focused on a village outside London and its protagonist, a simpleton called Barnaby Rudge. The novel was serialized in *Master Humphrey's Clock* from 1840 to 1841, and met with a lukewarm reception from the reading public, who thirsted for more novels in the vein of *The Old Curiosity Shop*.

Martin Chuzzlewit

Dickens therefore gave up on the historical genre, and began serializing the more picaresque *Martin Chuzzlewit* from December 1842 to June 1844. The book explores self-ishness and its consequences: the eponymous protagonist is the grandson and heir of the wealthy Martin Chuzzlewit senior, and is surrounded by relatives eager to inherit his money. But when Chuzzlewit junior finds himself disinherited and penniless, he has to make his own way in the world. Although it was a step forwards in his writing, being the first of his works to be written with a fully predetermined overall design, it sold poorly – partly due to the fact that publishing in general was experiencing a slump in the early 1840s. In a bid to revive sales, Dickens adjusted the plot during the serialization and sent the title character to America – his own recent visit there providing much material.

Christmas Books and The Haunted House

In 1843, Dickens had the idea of writing a small seasonal Christmas book, which would aim to revive the spirit of the holiday and address the social problems that he was increasingly interested in. The resulting work, *A Christmas Carol*, was a phenomenal success at the time, and the tale and its characters, such as Scrooge, Bob Cratchit and Tiny Tim, have now achieved an iconic status. Thackeray famously praised it as "a national benefit and to every man or woman who reads it a personal kindness". Dickens published four more annual Christmas novellas – *The Chimes*, *The Cricket on the Hearth*, *The Battle of Life* and *The Haunted Man* – which were successful at the time, but did not quite live up to the classic appeal of *A Christmas Carol*. After *The Haunted Man*, Dickens discontinued his Christmas books, but he included annual Christmas stories in his magazines *Household Words* and *All the Year Round*. Each set of these stories usually took the form of a miniature *Arabian Nights*, with a number of unrelated short stories linked together through a frame narrative – typically Dickens wrote the frame narrative, and invited other writers to supply the stories included within it, writing the occasional one of them himself. *The Haunted House* appeared in *All the Year Round* in 1862.

Dombey and Son

While living in Lausanne, Dickens composed *Dombey and Son*, which was serialized between October 1846 and April 1848 by Bradbury and Evans with highly successful results. The novel centres on Paul Dombey, the wealthy owner of a shipping company, who desperately wants a son to take over his business after his death. Unfortunately his wife dies giving birth to the longed-for successor, Paul Dombey junior, a sickly child who does not survive long. Although Dombey – who neglects his fatherly responsibilities towards his daughter Florence – is for the most part unsympathetic, he ends up turning a new leaf and becoming a devoted family man. Significantly, this is the first of Dickens's novels for which his working notes survive, from which one can clearly see the great care and detail with which he planned the novel.

David Copperfield (1849–1850) is at once the most per- *David Copperfield*
sonal and the most popular of Dickens's novels. He had tried, probably during 1847–48, to write his autobiography, but, according to his own later account, had found writing about certain aspects, such as his first love for Maria Beadnell, too painful. Instead he chose to transpose autobiographical events into a first-person *Bildungsroman*, *David Copperfield*, which drew on his personal experience of the blacking factory, journalism, his schooling at Wellington House and his love for Maria. Its depiction of the Micawbers owed much to Dickens's own parents. There was great critical acclaim for the novel, and it soon became widely held to be his greatest work.

For his next novel, *Bleak House* (1852–53), Dickens turned *Bleak House*
his satirical gaze on the English legal system. The focus of the novel is a long-running court case, Jarndyce and Jarndyce, the consequences of which reach from the filthy slums to the landed aristocracy. The scope of the novel may well be the broadest of all of his works, and Dickens also experimented with dual narrators, one in the third person and one in the first. He was well equipped to write on the subject matter due to his experiences as a law clerk and journalist, and his critique of the judiciary system was met with recognition by those involved in it, which helped set the stage for its reform in the 1870s.

Hard Times was Dickens's next novel, serialized in *House-* *Hard Times*
hold Words between April and August 1854, in which he satirically probed into social and economic issues to a degree not achieved in his other works. Using the infamous characters Thomas Gradgrind and Josiah Bounderby, he attacks utilitarianism, workers' conditions in factories, spurious usage of statistics and fact as opposed to imagination. The story is set in the fictitious northern industrial setting of Coketown, among the workers, school pupils and teachers. The shortest

and most polemical of Dickens's major novels, it sold extremely well on publication, but has only recently been fully accepted into the canon of Dickens's most significant works.

Little Dorrit   *Little Dorrit* (1855–57) was also a darkly critical novel, satirizing the shortcomings of the government and society, with institutions such as debtor's prisons – in one of which, as seen above, Dickens's own father had been held – and the fantastically named Circumlocution Office bearing the brunt of Dickens's bile. The plot centres on the romance which develops between the characters of Little Dorrit, a paragon of virtue who has grown up in prison, and Arthur Clennam, a hapless middle-aged man who returns to England to make a living for himself after many years abroad. Although at the time many critics were hostile to the work, taking issue with what they saw as an overly convoluted plot and a lack of humour, sales were outstanding and the novel is now ranked as one of Dickens's finest.

A Tale of Two Cities   *A Tale of Two Cities* is the second of Dickens's historical novels, covering the period between 1775 and 1793, from the American Revolution until the middle of the French Revolution. His primary source was Thomas Carlyle's *The French Revolution*. The story is of two men – Charles Darnay and Sydney Carton – who look very similar, though they are utterly different in character, who both love the same woman, Lucie Manette. The opening and closing sentences are among the most famous in literature: "It was the best of times, it was the worst of times." "It is a far, far better thing that I do, than I have ever done; it is a far, far better rest that I go to than I have ever known."

Great Expectations   Due to a slump in circulation figures for *All the Year Round*, Dickens brought out his next novel, in December 1860, as a weekly serial in the magazine, instead of having it published in monthly instalments as initially intended. The sales promptly recovered, and the audience and critics were delighted to read the story which some regard as Dickens's greatest ever work, *Great Expectations* (1860–61). On publication, it was immediately acclaimed a masterpiece, and was hugely successful in America as well as England. Like *David Copperfield*, it was written in the first person as a *Bildungsroman*, though this time its protagonist, Pip, was explicitly working class. Graham Greene once commented: "Dickens had somehow miraculously varied his tone, but when I tried to analyse his success, I felt like a colour-blind man trying intellectually to distinguish one colour from another." George Orwell was moved to declare: "Psychologically the latter part of *Great Expectations* is about the best thing Dickens ever did."

Dickens started work on his next novel, *Our Mutual Friend* (1864–65), by 1861 at the latest. It had an unusually long gestation period, and a mixed reception when first published. However, in recent years it has been reappraised as one of his greatest works. It is probably his most challenging and complicated, although some critics, including G.K. Chesterton, have argued that the ending is rushed. It opens with a young man on his way to receive his inheritance, which he can apparently only attain if he marries a beautiful and mercenary girl, Bella Wilfer, whom he has never met. However, before he arrives, a body is found in the Thames, which is identified as being him. So instead the money passes on to the Boffins, the effects of which spread through to various parts of London society.

Our Mutual Friend

In April 1870, the first instalment of Dickens's last novel, *The Mystery of Edwin Drood*, appeared. It was the culmination of Dickens's lifelong fascination with murderers. It was favourably received, outselling *Our Mutual Friend*, but only six of the projected twelve instalments were published, as Dickens died in June of that year.

The Mystery of Edwin Drood

There has naturally been much speculation on how the book would have finished, and suggestions as to how it should end. As it stands, the novel is set in the fictional area of Cloisterham, which is a thinly veiled rendering of Rochester. The plot mainly focuses on the choirmaster and opium addict John Jasper, who is in love with Rosa Bud – his pupil and his nephew Edwin Drood's fiancée. The twins Helena and Neville Landless arrive in Cloisterham, and Neville is attracted to Rosa Bud. Neville and Edwin end up having a huge row one day, after which Neville leaves town, and Edwin vanishes. Neville is questioned about Edwin's disappearance, and John Jasper accuses him of murder.

Select Bibliography

Biographies:
Ackroyd, Peter, *Dickens* (London: Sinclair-Stevenson, 1990)
Forster, John, *The Life of Charles Dickens* (London: Cecil Palmer, 1872–74)
James, Elizabeth, *Charles Dickens* (London: British Library, 2004)

Kaplan, Fred, *Dickens: A Biography* (London: Hodder & Stoughton, 1988)

Smiley, Jane, *Charles Dickens* (London: Weidenfeld and Nicolson, 2002)

Additional Recommended Background Material:
Collins, Philip, ed., *Dickens: The Critical Heritage* (London: Routledge & Kegan Paul, 1971)

Fielding, K.J, *Charles Dickens: A Critical Introduction* 2nd ed. (London: Longmans, 1965)

Wilson, Angus, *The World of Charles Dickens* (London: Secker & Warburg, 1970)

On the Web:
dickens.stanford.edu
dickens.ucsc.edu
www.dickensmuseum.com

ALMA CLASSICS

ALMA CLASSICS aims to publish mainstream and lesser-known European classics in an innovative and striking way, while employing the highest editorial and production standards. By way of a unique approach the range offers much more, both visually and textually, than readers have come to expect from contemporary classics publishing.

⌒

1. James Hanley, *Boy*
2. D.H. Lawrence, *The First Women in Love*
3. Charlotte Brontë, *Jane Eyre*
4. Jane Austen, *Pride and Prejudice*
5. Emily Brontë, *Wuthering Heights*
6. Anton Chekhov, *Sakhalin Island*
7. Giuseppe Gioacchino Belli, *Sonnets*
8. Jack Kerouac, *Beat Generation*
9. Charles Dickens, *Great Expectations*
10. Jane Austen, *Emma*
11. Wilkie Collins, *The Moonstone*
12. D.H. Lawrence, *The Second Lady Chatterley's Lover*
13. Jonathan Swift, *The Benefit of Farting Explained*
14. Anonymous, *Dirty Limericks*
15. Henry Miller, *The World of Sex*
16. Jeremias Gotthelf, *The Black Spider*
17. Oscar Wilde, *The Picture Of Dorian Gray*
18. Erasmus, *Praise of Folly*
19. Henry Miller, *Quiet Days in Clichy*
20. Cecco Angiolieri, *Sonnets*
21. Fyodor Dostoevsky, *Humiliated and Insulted*
22. Jane Austen, *Sense and Sensibility*
23. Theodor Storm, *Immensee*
24. Ugo Foscolo, *Sepulchres*
25. Boileau, *Art of Poetry*
26. Georg Kaiser, *Plays Vol. 1*
27. Émile Zola, *Ladies' Delight*
28. D.H. Lawrence, *Selected Letters*

To order any of our titles and for up-to-date information about our current and forthcoming publications, please visit our website on:

www.almaclassics.com